A Moment in Time

JENNIFER BACIA

 HarperCollins*Publishers*

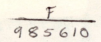

F
985610

HarperCollins*Publishers*

First published in Australia in 1996

Copyright © Jennifer Bacia 1996

HarperCollins*Publishers*
25 Ryde Road, Pymble, Sydney NSW 2073, Australia
31 View Road, Glenfield, Auckland 10, New Zealand
77–85 Fulham Palace Road, London W6 8JB, United Kingdom
Hazelton Lanes, 55 Avenue Road, Suite 2900, Toronto, Ontario M5R 3L2
and 1995 Markham Road, Scarborough, Ontario M1B 5M8, Canada
10 East 53rd Street, New York NY 10032, USA

National Library of Australia Cataloguing-in-publication data:
Bacia, Jennifer
  A moment in time
  ISBN 07322 5602 X
  I. Title.
A823.3

Cover: main photograph by Brian Geach, Hunter Valley landscape by
Oliver Strewe, cityscape by Kerry Klinner
Cover design by Darian Causby

Printed in Australia by Griffin Paperbacks, Adelaide

7 6 5 4 3 2 1
99 98 97 96

With love for John
who was so sure from the beginning
there'd be a happy ending.

Acknowledgements

For many of the themes of this book I am indebted to those wonderful women friends who shared with me their laughter and tears, failures and triumphs, strength and dreams. For their support and loving friendship I thank Tay, Helen, Donna, Caron, Suzanne, Jennifer, Lynda, Meryl, Jackie, Lynne, Tess, Iva, Helen and Lyn.

And, as always, my love and gratitude to Selwa Anthony – literary agent, wise woman, and wonderful friend – who believed in me every step of the long and difficult road.

CHAPTER ONE

We have no way of knowing when we wake to the day, the hour, that will change our lives. There is nothing that whispers to us: This is the moment in time. Life has no early warning system.

That morning Madeline Tyler rose taking life on trust as usual. She was an attractive, fair-haired woman of forty-two – though in her mind she still thought of herself as a girl. She was petite, slim, though not firm – at least not by the standards women set for themselves these days. Maddy Tyler's idea of fitness had been to give up cigarettes on her twenty-fifth birthday. It was nervous energy and self-discipline that kept her thin. She had a bony, interesting face and grey-blue eyes that had gradually lost their open frankness of twenty years before. These days they were a little dulled by the membrane of caution and disillusion.

Maddy Tyler's forty-two years had not been without their trials.

But she knew how to pretend, hiding behind her wit and sharp humour, her Zampatti wardrobe, her coolly contemporary home and well-documented success. Her CV was impressive but easily abridged – art gallery owner at twenty-seven, a concrete box she'd painted white in the heart of still-dangerous Surry Hills. It had been the perfect setting for art with an edge: individualistic, ambitious, obsessive. Like Maddy Tyler herself. Confident, driven, outspoken, she had known how to get attention. Art business is show business, she used to say. Put on a decent show and you'll get an audience.

By the time, four years later, that the Tyler Gallery had moved around the corner into a three-storey disused factory, Surry Hills was fast becoming the place to be for artists and dealers alike. And Maddy Tyler was already a name.

She was still in the same location. Had converted the top floor of the building into spacious open-plan living, the high off-white concrete walls a backdrop for paintings, rugs, sculpture, books, ceramics and tribal art. The bedroom was divided off, but only by a corral of antique Chinese screens. It was a long time since Maddy had last had to share her personal space, and privacy was not an issue.

The morning sun was streaming into the unfussy streamlined kitchen as she poured her first strong black coffee. The chipped ceramic mug was the only survivor from a set of six that had been a wedding present. Maddy's reluctance to discard this remnant of a previous existence was based on a too obvious nostalgia.

Her four years of married life seemed a lifetime away. She'd been twenty-one. Alex had been the third man she'd slept with. And the wedding was the sort that people had in those days – planned to the nth degree, overdressed relatives she barely knew, the honeymoon to Surfers.

Musing on it now brought a smile to her lips. The sort of smile that nurses something else in its fragile curve.

It was never easy to think of Alex. They had loved each other wholly and completely. From their first meeting each had recognised in the other the end of their longing. The heady feeling of completeness, the deep inner sigh that signals the heart's peace.

Sometimes, very occasionally, when she was feeling brave, Maddy would test herself to see if she could still remember how it had felt to love like that. The rush of joy when they met after even a few hours apart, the honest expression of feelings and thoughts, the feverish, endless sex, the sense of protection and security.

But now and then, despite her best efforts, Maddy's memories would push past the blockade she'd struggled to make emotion-tight. And she would remember how their short life together had ended. The fever and fatigue, the tests and pills, the shock and numbness when their questions had finally been answered.

It had taken six agonising months for the leukemia to eat out his brain, his blood, his marrow. During that time only the two of them had existed. Cocooned in the room she filled with their art, books and music, love and courage. Selfishly, greedily, compacting the rest of their lives into that savagely truncated time.

He died in her arms, his wasted cheeks paling against her breast. And in that last breathless moment her young husband's dark eyes had suddenly lit with something that transcended pain, that seemed to tell her he was going, but would be with her always.

She kept those bed sheets and had them still. Unwashed, wrapped in the dark, trapping his essence, his scent, his final moments. Only once, ten years afterwards, had she dared to take them out, hold them to her face, try to capture his soul. But the price had been too high and she had never done it again.

No one, she knew, would ever replace Alex. He had been her connection to her own spirit and soul. Everything she needed she had found in him.

But his death had also left her the legacy of impatient ambition. At college they had dreamed of the gallery they would one day own together, a place where talent might be nurtured, exposed, developed. And their plans had been steadily taking shape when fate had stamped its terrible, irrational foot.

Yet later, when Maddy was surprised to see that the sun still rose and faded, that the world barely noticed that one of its best had gone, she knew she had to do alone what they had planned to do together. The gallery became her obsession and her mission.

Many times during those first few years it had been touch and go. Her father's small inheritance had given her her start but she had often felt the hot breath of financial pressures and fifteen hour working days and seven day weeks became her norm.

And little had changed, she thought now as she sipped at her coffee. Already this year she'd fitted in half a dozen frantic overseas and interstate trips around a record number of exhibitions. And her usual hectic social life offered little respite from the pace. But that was the way Maddy liked it.

And this was success, she guessed, looking around her home. Modern, sleek, stylish, though not quite the haven it should be, with her business operating on the floors below. Financial realities had necessitated that arrangement at the start but now when she could afford a separate home she was reluctant to make the move. The gallery was her passion, her obsession and she accepted the difficulties in drawing the line between work and home. That was always a problem when you loved what you did, and hated to delegate. Perfectionism has its price.

Tonight's exhibition for example. A frantic race to get together the work of two – as yet – unknown talents she had championed and nurtured through the highs and lows of the creative process. Stroking egos, boosting confidence, playing therapist, priest, mother, legal and financial adviser. Exhausting . . . But exhilarating too, when she pulled it off.

Maddy rinsed the chipped mug and carefully turned it upside down on the draining board. Her artists were her family, her emotional release.

They were all she had.

The day passed quickly with the flurry of last minute hitches that were the usual prelude to any opening. At five, Tony Rabin, her right-hand man, shooed her upstairs. 'Off you go, Maddy, do the glam bit. *Trust* me. I can manage. Even if that ferret Lusko does arrive early.' Tim Lusko was one of the country's most acerbic critics.

Turning, Maddy pointed an index finger at Tony from halfway up the staircase. 'Bollinger. Three glasses in rapid succession is the best way to handle Lusko.'

'And you in something tight and red.'

She wrinkled her nose and gave him a self-deprecating smile. 'Does it work after forty?'

'Double my salary, sweetheart, and I'll flatter you incessantly.'

With a laugh Maddy continued up the stairs wondering again why it was only gay men she got on with these days.

Answer. Because she only ever mixed with gays. It was hard enough to meet someone straight, sane and available in the real world, never mind the art scene.

Oh, Maddy, she chided herself. *Meet* someone? She didn't think like that any more. Hadn't for years. She'd long ago resigned herself to never feeling that same passion and completeness – that selfless all-encompassing love – with anyone again.

She had dated, had lovers – too many – but no one had eased the longing she felt inside. In time she'd been forced to see that despite her silent denials she *was* searching for another Alex. As if miracles happened twice in the one lifetime . . .

Maddy Tyler was old enough to know that luck and joy are rationed and she'd had her share. But company, companionship – she'd allowed herself to hope for that. Gradually though she'd been forced to recognise that what she wanted didn't exist. It was what almost every other single woman in the country was looking for too. Someone tall, handsome, successful, sophisticated and cultured, confident and sensitive, compassionate, kind. The half dozen males in the country that fitted that description, she mused wryly, had been tagged long ago. And they were far too sensitive, compassionate and kind to ever dream of leaving their very happy wives . . .

She took a quick shower, then stood in front of the silver framed mirror and re-did her face. There were lines that hadn't been there just six months ago and she etched them deeper with her frown of recognition.

Why should age matter? she asked herself. But it did. And it was always worse for women. If Maddy was grateful for anything it was that looks weren't all she had to sustain her. She had other means of power – money, talent, influence. The sorts of things men respected in each other. The things that made life easier – and sometimes harder. If you were a woman.

Maddy wondered, as she did more often these days, what happened to truly beautiful women when their beauty flaked and dried and crumpled. Did their sense of self survive?

There was surgery of course. The baby boomers with money could take that option. She might even be tempted herself – if she could only decide whether she was doing it for herself, or for some man, as yet unknown, who would love her for her pretty, youthful face. For wasn't that what men noticed and wanted most of all?

Maddy's blue-grey eyes beamed their cynical light. No man had ever told her that her brain – or her heart – turned him on.

Twenty minutes later the first guests were just beginning to arrive, Joel and Alice Sherman among them. The Shermans were one of her core of rich, urbane collectors who bought from the heart while trusting Maddy's judgement, and she greeted them with professional warmth.

By seven the room was a mass of bodies. Street Cred brushing shoulders with Couture, Maddy moving like a dervish from group to group – collectors, artists, clients, media. She loved the challenge of selling – especially when something was difficult to sell. Many of the serious collectors had made their purchases at an earlier private showing and were here tonight to relish the buzz and the satisfying knowledge of their own supremacy.

As Maddy spun around the room one of the two featured artists managed to pin her down. His dope-striped eyes looked out from a sweaty, nervous face. 'I saw the Kilbys looking at *Vivid Two*, but they moved away. Do you think they –?'

She interrupted him. 'They'll take it, Rees, I promise.' His insecurity faded under her reassurance and with a smile she moved on.

'Maddy . . .'

She turned in response to the tap on her arm and her face lit in welcome.

'Luke! I'm so glad you could make it.' She looked past the slim, dark-haired man with his neatly trimmed beard. 'Is Neville –?'

Luke Allen shook his head, his eyes suddenly shaded with pain. 'One of his bad days, Maddy. I can't leave him too long. But he wanted me to drop in and see how things were going.' He looked away. 'It's easy to lose touch with people when . . .'

Instinctively Maddy reached for his hand. 'I'm here for you any time, Luke, for you both. Please know that. Don't feel you have to face this alone.'

The young man nodded, his dark eyes swimming with tears. 'Thanks. Thanks Maddy. Neville said to give you a hug for him.'

Her eyes clouded. Neville Harper had been one of her most promising young artists until he too had fallen victim to the plague that was scything so ruthlessly through the ranks of talented gay men. She'd been devastated when she'd first heard the news that his HIV status had progressed to full-blown AIDS but had encouraged the ailing artist to keep working as long as he was able.

For Maddy Tyler had long ago learned the value of the balm of work.

It was ten minutes later that she received the first warning. But she chose to ignore it. The room was hot, overcrowded, that was all.

Then the pain stabbed at her again. And this time Maddy felt nauseous, dizzy, as if she were going to faint. Recovering slightly, she interrupted her conversation with a quick excuse and made for the powder room at the foot of the stairs.

The waves of pain returned, were shooting up her arm and neck. Panting, she gripped the sides of the vanity and was startled by her reflection in the mirror. Grey, clammy cheeks, hair sticking damply to her forehead. What was the matter with her? She was never sick, prided herself on her energy and stamina.

It was one of the female guests who found her. Slumped on the tiled floor. A doctor was plucked from the crush and a white-faced Tony frantically dialled triple 0.

The day, the hour had arrived. But, like the rest of us, Maddy Tyler hadn't had a clue.

And that was only the beginning.

CHAPTER TWO

'Maddy, I *insist*! It's exactly what you need. A total break. Away from everything. It's yours for as long as you want. Bill and I are going to be in Oxford for at least a year.'

'Clare, it's very kind, really. But a few days up north somewhere is –'

Her friend stared down at her in agitated disbelief. 'A few *days*! Maddy, hasn't it sunk in? You've had a coronary! At forty-*two*. A couple of days in some overcrowded tourist hang-out isn't going to do you any damn good. You need peace, tranquillity, a total rest. Exactly what you'll get at "Field House".'

From where she sat propped up in her hospital bed, Maddy understood the concern and caring that lay behind Clare Ingram's fiery manner. Her friends had been truly wonderful these last three weeks. And Maddy still needed all the help she could get to come to terms with what had happened. A blocked coronary artery that might have taken her life.

The three days of crisis, when she had lain in intensive care rigged up like a ship under sail, remained a vague memory. But how she had hated being dependent on the parade of eager, bustling professionals who seemed never to leave her a moment alone.

She'd had to stop herself shrugging off helping hands, bite back her irritation at their too cheerful encouragement as she took her first faltering steps around the ward.

'It'll take time, Miss Tyler. Just be patient. You'll get there.'

Later, slumped against her pillows, sweating and breathless from the effort of moving cottonwool legs, Maddy had found herself fighting back tears.

She kept asking herself incessantly how this could have happened to *her*? Women of her age didn't have heart attacks! Wasn't forty-two meant to be the prime of life? And they expected her to be patient and pleased at managing half a dozen wobbly steps when she was used to operating at a hundred miles an hour. Making things happen. Being in charge, control.

It was the realisation that her body had let her down that shocked Maddy the most. She, who had thought herself so healthy and invincible – non-smoker, light drinker, not overweight. As she lay trapped between the tight, sanitised sheets she found herself focusing fearfully on the soft, fist-sized pump that sat only centimetres beneath her breast. Its every beat now reminding her of her vulnerability, the ephemeral slightness of the Now.

The specialist had used words like 'fortunate' and 'very lucky'. She'd had a warning, he said. 'Heredity's not on your side given your father's early death, Ms Tyler, but taking into account your other low risk factors stress must certainly have played a part. The fact is you're going to have to make some changes in your lifestyle.'

Changes. Maddy hated changes. And the demands of her routine suited her. Twelve or fourteen hour days. Sunday little different from Tuesday or Friday. Immersed in work she thoroughly enjoyed.

Or, suddenly with time to ponder she found herself ambushed by the thought, working so hard – even when she didn't need to – because there was nothing – or no one – else to absorb her emotional energy?

Canvas in place of a body. Meetings in place of a mate. With a grimace she turned cynical, weary eyes to the creamy nothingness of the hospital wall. Sure. Easy. Tomorrow she'd just demand a prescription for love.

Her recovery progressed and she'd settled back into her apartment, but the sudden confrontation with her own mortality left Maddy unable to shrug off the straitjacket of depression. For the first time in years she felt unsettled, afraid and vulnerable, no longer sure of the future.

Admitting to such unfamiliar emotional turmoil forced her to acknowledge the wisdom of her doctor's advice. She would have to do something about certain aspects of her life.

'I'm delighted you changed your mind, Maddy! You'll adore the place. We always come back to Sydney feeling completely relaxed – and asking ourselves why we don't get up here more often.'

Maddy was sitting in the passenger seat of Clare Ingram's BMW as they bounced in a cloud of dust over the unsealed road from Paynes Crossing. Having acknowledged the need to get her health back on track she had seen the sense in accepting the Ingrams' generous offer of a couple of weeks at their country retreat. A total break in peace and quiet. Rest and recuperation.

Yet Maddy still couldn't help wondering if she wouldn't go crazy stuck out here on her own.

The country . . . Hell, she was a city girl, born and bred. Her father had run his small watch repair business within cooee of the Town Hall. Next door had been an artist's supply shop and it was among those dusty shelves of frames and canvases and tubes of exotically named paints that Maddy had first developed her interest in art.

The City was her natural habitat. She thrived on the ceaseless pace and noise and activity. For Maddy, movies and theatres and restaurants and shops were as necessary as nicotine or personal trainers to those of other compulsions.

'There's a whole library of books, magazines, videos,' Clare had countered some of her unspoken fears as she'd helped Maddy to pack. 'You won't be bored for a minute. And I'll give you all the neighbours' numbers and Mrs Cole's. She'll come and clean whenever you want – plus pick up anything you might need on her way out from town. And don't worry,' Clare had laughed, 'sun dried tomatoes and balsamic vinegar and most other foodie obsessions have made it to the Hunter Valley. You won't have to suffer any serious culinary deprivations.'

From the comfort of the car Maddy looked out at the surrounding countryside. The Hunter River area was one of Australia's premier wine-growing districts but just at the moment she couldn't see a sign of anything that looked like a grapevine. Just low rolling hills, dry spiky grass, peeling gums. The Australia of calendars. Of nothingness and boredom. Again she wondered how she was going to cope for two whole weeks.

At least it was usually a quiet time of year at the gallery. Tony could easily hold the fort. But still, Maddy hated not having her hands on the reins. Being in charge. It was her modus operandi. The way she had lived her life for so long. And who knew what might go wrong in a fortnight?

'Here we are!' Clare's voice interrupted her thoughts as the car slowed down and they turned into a driveway marked by the ubiquitous milk can mailbox. A professionally painted sign on the wire fence read Field House.

The BMW lurched over the cattle grid, then a few metres on the track curved to the right and there was the house nestled among native shrubs and a cluster of gums.

'Clare, it's huge . . .' Maddy stared out at the long, brick colonial style building. A verandah, trimmed in some sort of creeper, ran its length and the shiny metal roof spouted four dormer windows and a chimney.

'Well, it was built to take Bill's kids as well as mine. There's nine of us altogether don't forget.' Clare had brought the car to a stop by the front steps and was opening her door. 'But don't worry about rattling around too much inside – it's really very cosy.'

Clare was right. Walls of river stone, wooden beams, and a scattering of richly coloured rugs gave the house a welcoming warmth. The living room walls and casual tables were covered in framed family photographs and a long comfortable sofa faced a large combustion fireplace. From french doors that opened onto the verandah Maddy could see cattle grazing in the distance.

Clare settled her in, showed her her room with its double brass bed and lace-trimmed curtains and gave her a quick guided tour of the rest of the house. A glance in the refrigerator revealed that Maddy was in no danger of starving.

'And here,' Clare opened a narrow door at the far end of the hall, 'is Bill's pride and joy.'

Maddy saw the short flight of steps leading downwards.

Clare grinned. 'The cellar. And don't forget a couple of glasses a day are supposed to be great for the heart. So help yourself. A lot of local stuff of course.'

In the shed out the back was a dusty ute and Clare climbed into the driver's seat, turned the key, and gave a satisfied nod as the engine kicked into life. 'Mrs C turns it over for us regularly,' she explained. Then switching off the motor she dropped the key in Maddy's palm. 'All yours.'

Half an hour later Maddy stood watching the BMW disappear and wondered just how she was going to stand the utter silence.

It took her four days to overcome the unease of displacement. At first restless and disoriented she found it almost impossible to sit and do nothing more than read a book or listen to music. She began to realise that there were different kinds of addictions. In her case she was faced with withdrawing from the drug of near constant human contact and the adrenalin rush of business.

It took willpower not to succumb to the tempting proximity of the telephone. Her sense of isolation would only be made worse by talking to friends in Sydney. And in Tony's case, he'd be miffed, she knew, at the thought that she didn't trust him to cope for a mere couple of weeks.

He'd promised to call if there was anything absolutely vital they needed to discuss.

Re-establishing the human need for habit and routine, Maddy rose early, cooked simple meals, took her medication and did an hour's daily walking as instructed by her doctor – always with an eye to any lurking wildlife. By evening, bored by television and easily tired, she went to bed early with a book.

She soon learned that the so-called total silence of the country was a myth. To begin with, the various solos and symphonies had taken some getting used to – especially at night. The scuttles and scamperings, the dry rustles, the sonorous hoots and high-pitched chatterings. Distracted from the printed page she would remain perfectly still, listening and wondering what creature, harmless or lethal, was threatening invasion.

Then, gradually, she became familiar with the scratch of bird claws on the metal roof, the dry crackle of wind through gum trees, the distant moan of cattle. She began enjoying the gentle warmth of the sun against her arms and the tang of different scents as she took her daily walk around the perimeter of the paddocks.

It came as a surprise to feel the change taking place within her. As if some tight screw were being slowly unwound so that even her bones seemed to soften and relax. For the first time she began to realise the extent of the tension and pressure she had accepted as the norm in her daily existence. The striving for perfection, the chasing of deadlines, the manic drive of the Career Woman incarnate.

And now that she understood the toll that had been exacted on her health Maddy was determined to ease up on herself. Somehow.

As her addiction to human contact decreased it was easily met by the odd trip into the local village for fresh bread and fruit, and the occasional visit by Mrs Cole, the local who looked after the house for the Ingrams. But much as she enjoyed the exchange with the cheerful, bustling woman who swept around the house with her dusters and brooms and cleaning agents Maddy was glad when she was once again alone.

Occasionally she took the ute out on exploratory trips, to a couple of vineyards, the local towns. It was in Wollombi – population around five hundred, one main street – that she saw it. She was walking back to her parking spot with a milkshake and the *Sydney Morning Herald* in hand and paused to look in the flyblown window of the local real estate office. Vacant land, farms, homes in small hamlets at prices which wouldn't buy a garage in Sydney.

About to turn away it suddenly caught her eye. A faded photograph below eye level. Leaning closer, Maddy studied the small, tin-roofed wooden cottage, its front verandah heavily laced with greenery. Ten acres, two under vines, backs onto river. Near the village of Broke. A steal.

She looked at the price, recalled memories of Broke from one of her recent drives. Cafe, service station, two churches. A general store with a liquor licence in place of a pub.

Sipping the last of her milkshake, Maddy walked away. Three months ago she couldn't have imagined how anyone could have survived living in a place like Broke.

Solitude. Dusk. The orange pink flush on clouds as the day slid away. Dressed in jeans and a warm sweater Maddy sat on the faded swing seat on the Ingrams' verandah sipping at her glass of medicinal Semillon.

She thought of the arterial clog of cars on Broadway, Oxford Street, William Street. The deep throated 'Om' from a million exhausts. The expressions on the faces of the wage earners – as determined as explorers, as they hacked their way through the undergrowth of neon, litter, office politics, to the civilisation of their own living rooms. Set beside freeways, under flight paths, next to factories and treatment plants.

Closing her eyes she breathed in the sweetness of the dazed evening air. She could feel her solitude. Taste it. Hear it.

And at that precise moment, in a somersault of certainty, Maddy got a sense of the timeless, tensile bonds connecting her to the universe, of the knowledge that she had been born an elemental part of everything – from the first speck of light that had sprung from the unknown blackness of Before. And, for the first time in years, Maddy Tyler felt an overwhelming longing to love and be loved.

The darkness grew around her, choking her with the utter despair of certainty that that would never happen again.

CHAPTER THREE

'Da-rling! You're looking so well!'

'Maddy, how super to see you, sweetheart.'

Cheeks and lips performed their ritual brush-ings as she moved into the sea of familiar faces. The long, softly lit room was crowded. When Eric Kitzberg gave a party nobody who was nobody was there. A high-profile money market man astute enough to have survived the eighties brilliantly intact, Kitzberg was equally famous for his patronage of the arts. A collector of inter-national reputation, he was one of Maddy's most influential and colourful clients.

That evening at his multi-level harbourside home he was playing host to some of the country's best known names – artists, sculptors, writers, film-makers, reviewers – all partaking eagerly of the 'Bollinger, Beluga and bullshit' as Tony Rabin so succinctly put it to Maddy and others within earshot.

It was Maddy's first real social outing since her return from 'Field House' and she was met with both surprised comments at how well she looked and solicitous enquiries about the state of her health. There were those who had been as shocked as herself that equal rights could also extend to the male stress syndrome.

'Surely they haven't had you in hospital all this time, Maddy?' Jock Meekin, a portly, goateed writer munificently supported for years by Arts Council grants, blinked at her through puffy, champagne-friendly eyes.

'Don't worry, Jock, they didn't let me chew up your taxpayer dollar a moment longer than I had to. I just got away for a while.'

'We all *wondered* where you'd gone, darling.' Prue Marks, a large woman in floating layers of multicoloured chiffon was looking over Maddy's shoulder as she spoke. A noted ceramicist, she hated wasting a moment of such a perfect occasion when she could be extending her circle of wealthy clients.

Tony piped in, his tone teasing. 'We managed to force her out of town. And now I've proved she's utterly dispensable.'

'Where'd you go, darling? Hayman? Lizard?' Five star island resorts were considered Maddy Tyler's style.

Maddy smiled over the top of her crystal rim. 'The Hunter actually.'

Eyes widened. Bemused looks.

'*You*. In the sticks, Maddy?'

'Darling, how did you endure?'

Maddy raised an insouciant bare shoulder. 'Amazing what petrol-free air's got going for it.'

As she took in the unconvinced expressions of her city dweller acquaintances Maddy wondered what they'd say if they knew what was on her mind.

The idea had been borne of her overwhelming experience that evening on the Ingrams' darkening verandah. A sense of the spiritual, of being transformed. And Maddy had found herself left with a strange and desperate longing to feel that way again.

At ten o'clock people were still arriving but, already tiring, Maddy went in search of her host to offer her thanks and take her leave. It was while she was making her way to the cloakroom to pick up her purse that she came face to face with one of the new arrivals.

'Oh . . . Ken . . . How are you?'

Even though it was almost three years since their brief affair had ended, Ken Bristow looked as handsome as ever. It was his looks that had dazzled her when they'd been introduced at the dinner party of a mutual friend. Ken Bristow had a dark brooding attractiveness that had made her think of Pacino. She had always found that hint of danger rather appealing. As well, the Pacino look-alike was tall, languid, graceful, beautifully dressed – qualities which might have aroused her suspicions about his gender preference except for the fact that Maddy knew her host, Peter, had asked him especially for her to meet. And as she talked to the man across the table Maddy wondered if, in a lifetime of blind dates, she might actually have met the one who could be right.

Still, attracted as she was to the handsome, articulate lawyer, she was too wise and experienced to fall for any man on the basis of good looks and a smooth tongue. Yet, as the night progressed, Maddy found herself unable to resist working through her usual mental checklist: Sophisticated, check. Cultured, check. Confident. Successful. He was even the right age – three years older than herself. And on top of all that there was his unlawyer-like knowledge of the arts. Friend of the AO, enjoyed modern dance as well as ballet, read Roth and Carey, skied Aspen, holidayed in Italy or France. And – she felt the effervescence dance through her veins – Ken Bristow even had a sense of humour.

Maddy could hardly believe her luck. Discarding her reservations with untypical haste she moved full tilt into witty, sophisticated, successful female mode. Someone who didn't *need* a man. Wasn't *looking*.

But was quite happy to be found . . .

When he'd asked for her number at the end of the evening she'd wondered fleetingly whether to play hard to get. Put him lightly off while hinting at the possibility of success if he persisted. Wasn't that supposed to make a man more eager? But the gleaming female eyes spotlighting this rare male specimen from various sittings around the table had alerted her to the risks. She'd smiled and given him her card.

Later that night as she drove herself home Maddy had felt a quickening in her throat every time she remembered a smile, a gesture, a snippet of their witty conversation.

Ken Bristow was everything she was looking for.

Even though she wasn't looking.

'How've you been, Maddy?' He was giving her the ex-girlfriend smile. The 'aren't you lucky you had me even for a little while' one.

'I –' But there was no point in telling him what had happened. She didn't want his polite sympathy. Ken Bristow had never really been interested in anyone else but himself.

'I never complain, Ken. And you? Taking to fatherhood as well as Warren and Jack?'

He'd married eighteen months ago – a red-headed model type twenty years his junior. The baby had come along exactly ten months later. The late life options of the male.

'Vicky's a natural.'

Good lawyer answer. Non-answer.

'She's not with you?' Maddy asked with sweet provocativeness.

'It's difficult . . . sometimes for us both to –' He trailed off looking now as if he wished he hadn't stopped to speak.

Maddy flashed him a wide smile. 'I'm sure.'

'See you around then, Maddy. Glad everything's going well.' He brushed past her, heading to a world far away from breast milk and mushy nappies.

But Maddy had one final question. For old times sake — always the sentimentalist. 'Political career still on the agenda, Ken?'

He stopped and looked back over his shoulder, surprised.

He'd probably forgotten he'd ever shared that one with her. She remembered how, one evening after they'd made love, he'd told her about his political ambitions. And then: 'Do you think I'm too good looking to be Prime Minister, Maddy?' It had taken her a moment or two to realise he wasn't joking. Then, left breathless by the unashamed revelation of ego, she realised she couldn't go on fooling herself any longer.

'The law's been good to me, Maddy,' he was answering her seriously, 'but I haven't ruled that option out. No, not yet.'

'Good luck, Ken.'

She turned and moved on, feeling nothing. Except maybe a faint distaste that she had ever allowed herself to be dazzled, no matter for how short a time, by someone like Ken Bristow.

The thought stayed with her as she drove home, glad to be on her own if that was the alternative. Their affair had lasted three months until reality had settled like cream from her illusions. Ken had been an art form, a study in fastidiousness. From

the Gucci wet bag and towelling robe – comple-
ments of the Bangkok Oriental – to the solid gold
egg timer for his morning eggs.

Everything about him had been impeccable –
his apartment, his taste in music and socks, even
his lovemaking. Yet he'd only grudgingly agreed
when she'd insisted on an AIDS test for both of
them before the first time. As if he considered it
an insult to suggest that a man as neat and clean as
he could be any risk.

Afterwards Maddy wondered why she'd both-
ered for the sex had been utterly lacking in
passion or rawness. His breathing had barely got
heavier – in case, she mused, he might disturb his
nasal hair?

She remembered too the expression on his face
the morning she'd once inadvertently presented
him with the chipped coffee mug. Lips pursed.
Frown. 'I'd get rid of this one, Maddy.'

She had looked back into that too handsome
face. 'You're right,' she'd answered pointedly, 'it's
long overdue.'

And then the difficulty of readjusting to singledom again. Even a self-centred narcissist like Ken
Bristow became a habit after a while. And that
was the danger. Enduring something that wasn't
right, would never be right, because it kept you in
step with the rest of the human race. Coupledom.
Someone to wake up with on Sunday morning.
Who irritated you for the rest of the week . . .

And since Ken Bristow there had been nobody else. She had opted out. Admitted the total impossibility of ever meeting anyone who would be able to make her soul and heart and body sing as Alex had. Oh, no, these days Maddy Tyler was not a contender.

She drove into her underground garage, keeping an eye out to ensure no one slipped in before the security door closed. The sharpened senses of the city dweller. As she took the small service elevator up to her apartment Maddy felt the bite of a familiar loneliness. Accepted now, but her constant companion.

Yet still better than Australia's most handsome PM.

She was surprised at how quickly and easily she made the decision. The longing for what she'd experienced that evening at 'Field House' had not gone away. And one Saturday morning a short time after her return to the city she again made the journey north to Wollombi.

With a sense of relief she found the advertisement still in the grimy front window. The agent, a gregarious, freckle-faced man in his thirties, drove her in his dusty, non-airconditioned Ford to inspect the place.

Less than two hours later the deal was done.

Five weeks later Maddy made the trip north again, her Saab packed with linen, crockery and provisions. The sale had gone through without a hitch. The aged owner had passed away in a Newcastle nursing home five months previously and the family had just wanted to get rid of the place, old-fashioned furniture and all. Sentiment meets mortgage and school fees.

She arrived mid-morning, bouncing over the grassy track, nervously eager to renew her acquaintance with a place she had seen only once before. Had she made too hasty a decision? Been seduced by some post-recuperative fantasy during that time at the Ingrams'?

But as she climbed the three rickety steps and stepped beneath the fringe of trailing vine, the remembered sense of peace and pleasure greeted her and she knew she had not made a mistake.

The front door offered the same cantankerous resistance as it had at that one and only inspection but finally Maddy stepped into the cool darkness of the hall. As she moved from room to room she noted with satisfaction that the able Mrs C hadn't let her down. Cobwebs, dust and grime had all been whisked away.

The furniture was forty years out of date – silky oak beds in each of the three bedrooms, a rather nice maple wardrobe with mirrored doors, and a heavy round dining table in knotted pine with chairs that didn't match. Not exactly Country Living Catalogue.

Maddy smiled. She'd enjoy making it her own, had seen the possibilities for renovation at once.

The cottage would be her retreat. A place to recover both physically and mentally. To put herself together so she could make it through the rest of her life . . .

She spent the day settling in, making a list of things to buy, of renovations that would need doing. The walls were tongue and groove. Painted pale blue they'd make a nice contrast to the floorboards once they were stripped and polished. The living room opened onto the verandah and featured a brick open fireplace similar to the one in the kitchen. The bathroom – a lean-to at the end of the verandah – was barely adequate, but she had figured it could easily be converted to an ensuite if a door was knocked through into the back bedroom. She'd add another loo and shower for guests.

That is, she smiled wryly, if she could persuade anyone she knew to drag themselves out of the city. Although the vineyards might help.

By late afternoon she was feeling tired and decided on a quick shower and an early dinner. Tomorrow when she'd had a good night's rest she'd explore outside a little more.

The shower was a large, rusty, mildew-dripping head over the high-sided, claw-footed tub. There was no curtain but it hardly mattered given the state of the peeling linoleum. Gingerly Maddy stepped out onto the shower mat and wrapped herself in one of her white Bloomingdale bath towels.

Hair damp around her face she dressed in jeans and sweat shirt and prepared something to eat in the shabby, old-fashioned kitchen. A new refrigerator would be an essential on her list. And next week she'd get the important things happening. Buy what she needed, ferret out local tradesmen.

Too tired to be very hungry, she settled for bread, cheese, fruit and a glass of wine. It was chilly but she wrapped herself in a warmer sweater and carried her plate and glass onto the verandah where the one weathered wicker chair remained.

Night had crept over the paddocks but she sat in a small pool of yellow light from the living room window, eating and listening to the same rustlings and chatterings she had grown used to at the Ingrams'.

And gradually, moment by moment the magic crept over her again. Lulling her blood. Soothing her mind. Calming her spirit. The house enclosing her like some holy sheltering grotto in the middle of flat, empty darkness.

And for a short space of time she didn't have to be Maddy, the driven, the successful, the independent. Here, alone, she could allow herself to touch those other strings inside herself – strum the melodies of vulnerability, loss, longing.

'Oh, Alex . . .' The whisper in her mind's ear. The blade-sharp desire for his presence . . .

As night coiled itself around her, Maddy Tyler replayed the slides of memory.

CHAPTER FOUR

City complexion protected by a wide brimmed hat, Maddy went exploring, the heels of her boots leaving depressions in the dusty earth that now belonged to her.

With the same proprietorial air she inspected what was left of the vegetable garden behind the house. Weeds sprouting amid a few parched rows, a straggly pumpkin vine, some clumps of what looked like cabbage and lettuce run to seed. Bending down in her slim-fitting jeans, she touched the crumbling soil with tentative fingers. She would bring it back to life. Would read books to find out what to do. Then grow things she had only ever picked off a supermarket shelf.

The thought warmed her with a quiet pleasure.

After lunch she got ready to leave, acknowledging the knot of resistance inside her. She wanted to stay longer, felt the need to allow the house and its surroundings to seep further into her senses, to establish more securely the balance she had been so graphically shown was missing in her life.

As she locked the cottage door and slid onto leather warmed by the sun, she also knew that this time she hadn't made a mistake. There had been too many in the past. Of one kind or another. And she had grown weary of learning the lessons they brought in their wake.

Barely a kilometer up the road Maddy knew something was seriously wrong. Her hands grew cold and clammy around the steering wheel. Her heart raced. Sweat bubbled on her forehead and she was swept by a wave of nausea.

Pulling over she brought the car to a skewed halt on the grassy verge and opened the door. Legs spread wide she bent over, waiting to be sick. Her hands were shaking, her body felt chilled and at the same time damp with sweat. Oh God. She'd pushed herself too hard, overdone things. Another attack.

Filled with dread, she knew that somehow she would have to get up and look for her pills packed with everything else in the back of the car. Yet at the moment she felt incapable of movement.

Only gradually did the approaching noise penetrate her tiny world of fear and pain. And then a voice – deep, tentative, solicitous.

'Are you okay? Need some help?'

Somehow Maddy managed to raise her head. A man. Tall. Greying dark hair under a sweat-stained, broad-brimmed hat. The lines in his sunburnt face etched deeper in concern. The tractor in the background.

'I – I'm not feeling very well . . .' She was trembling uncontrollably.

He strode forward, bent his lanky frame through the barbed wire fence. 'You'd better lie down a sec. I'm going to drive you to my place, okay? It's at the end of the track.'

She barely managed a nod but he was already levering her gently into the passenger seat, taking her place behind the wheel.

Ten minutes after slipping the Anginine beneath her tongue she was almost herself again. As she lay on the thin, hard divan in the sparsely furnished room, the stranger called Fraser O'Neill nodded down at her.

'Colour's coming back. You looked like a glass of milk there for a while. How d'you feel?' Such measured speech in place of city staccato.

'A million per cent.' Maddy still felt a little weak but the chills and nausea had passed and her heart seemed to be dancing to its normal tune.

She removed the damp folded facecloth from her forehead and handed it back. 'Thanks.'

Tentatively she sat up and swung her legs off the divan onto the bare wooden floorboards. Testing. A black and tan German Shepherd watching her from the corner, stirred and raised its head.

'I think I'm okay to drive now.'

'Want a cup of something before you go?'

She looked up at him and smiled. 'Well . . . I guess it's the neighbourly thing to do.'

His eyes were the colour of a mid-summer sky. They looked at her now with a quizzical expression. 'Don't tell me you're the lady who bought the Lancaster place?'

Maddy nodded. 'Moved in yesterday. Must've worn myself out with all this country air.'

He grinned as he crossed to the kitchen sink and held a battered electric jug under the tap. 'Yeah, you've gotta be careful around here. Dangerous place. Not like Sydney.'

And suddenly Maddy found herself laughing aloud.

Over a cup of instant coffee she made the discovery that Fraser O'Neill had once owned the house that now belonged to her. It was where he and his wife had lived when they were first married.

The O'Neills were one of the original farming families in the district, running dairy cattle on a couple of hundred acres that extended to the river flats. But times had grown tougher and it was Fraser who'd had to face the fact that, without sons to help him run the place, he couldn't go on.

'My daughter married and moved up the coast. Her husband wasn't interested in the place, and why should he be? He and Joy have their own lives. But dairying's too labour-intensive without family. Still, I tried to keep it going. That's when I sold off your house and land and a few other acres. But it wasn't enough. Had to sell the lot in the end. Now I lease the place from the wine-makers and grow their grapes for them.'

Maddy heard no hint in his voice of what it might have cost to lose property that had been his family's for generations. But it must have been hard, she thought, to start over at his age. Fraser O'Neill wasn't young. Fifty-something she guessed. His complexion had the patina of someone who had spent his life out of doors but his lean, fit looking body could have belonged to a man twenty years his junior. She studied him surreptitiously as he sat opposite her on the hard kitchen chair, long, slim, jeans-clad legs stretched out in front of him, weather roughened hands playing with his empty coffee mug, thick, cattle-dog coloured hair in need of a cut. Ruggedly attractive – if you liked the country type.

He asked her what she did in the city and she saw his frown when she told him. 'You mean you can make a decent living out of selling art?'

Maddy smiled and assured him it was possible.

'Must be stressful – to affect your health like that, I mean.' She'd had to tell him about what had happened.

Maddy shrugged, there wasn't much more she wanted to say about that. 'Maybe I should take up growing grapes.' She looked around for her car keys. It was time to go.

He gave her a lopsided grin. 'Well, the bank manager sure doesn't hassle me like he used to. Too old for all that at fifty-two.'

It was obvious money was still tight. The house had clearly once been a substantial family home.

Now it had a shabby, neglected air. There were the remnants of a few decent pieces of furniture and on the dusty chiffonier a large, framed studio portrait had pride of place. A woman, pretty, freckled, open faced, her dark hair crimped in tight waves. Perched on her knee was a chubby, ringleted baby in an old fashioned smocked dress.

His wife and daughter, Maddy supposed. Although judging by the state of the house it would appear he now lived alone.

She drove him back to his tractor. As he swung his long legs out of the car Maddy repeated her grateful thanks for the help and the coffee.

Leaning in at the open window, he smiled and lifted his well-worn hat in an old fashioned gesture. 'Nice to have a neighbour again. Let me know if you need anything. I'm never far away.'

As she drove away Maddy could tell that Fraser O'Neill would be a good neighbour.

Over the next three weeks, work kept her as busy as ever but she did her best not to overdo things. Most important of all she managed to squeeze in a couple of trips to the cottage – on both occasions to deal with the various local tradesmen recommended by the agent who had sold her the place.

At the end of that time the major renovations were complete and Maddy was more than happy with the result.

The bathroom was now tiled in white with a floor of handmade terracotta – although the tiler had seen fit to warn her about the marks and faded colouring on 'this second hand stuff'.

The tongue and groove walls were washed in pale blue, the floorboards stripped and polished and warmed here and there with earthy coloured kilims. The limed wooden cabinets for the kitchen had been made in Sydney and transported to the cottage along with a new refrigerator, cook top, and mattresses for the old-fashioned beds. And in the living room a cosy, down-filled sofa and three easy chairs semi-circled the fireplace.

Despite her earlier vow about an unhurried approach Maddy completed the major part of the make-over in only a slightly modified version of her usual high-octane style. Tradesmen, used to taking four days at some particular task, completed it in less than twenty four hours under their employer's energetic supervision.

For so long, full steam had been all Maddy knew. She ran, she told herself, so that in the end she could rest. But whereas in the past she had simply forgotten to stop running, now she understood the dangers to her health of overdoing things. She had had a warning and her deter-mined efforts, she excused herself, were aimed at having the cottage ready in time for Christmas. Then she would take a break and have nothing to do but relax.

On the second of her two visits to the cottage Fraser O'Neill dropped by. Maddy was in the kitchen supervising the installation of the cabinets and the arrival of the pick-up was masked by the high pitched screech of the sanding machine on the hall floorboards.

It was his shadow blocking out the sunlight that made her look up. And there he was, smiling at her from the doorway, lifting the same worn hat in greeting. It was hardly the best of times to be interrupted, but Maddy mouthed a friendly hullo and followed him outside, away from the noise.

They stood in the shade at the end of the verandah. The day was hot for mid-October and there were patches of sweat under the armholes of his faded denim shirt.

'Sorry to disturb you. Didn't have your phone number. Just thought I should let you know I'm going to be letting off the gas gun at the birds. Didn't want the noise worrying you.' He grinned and nodded towards the house. 'Guess I could have saved myself the trouble.'

'No. Thanks. He's almost finished. It was good of you to let me know. The birds give you a lot of trouble?'

'Yeah. This time of the year.' He looked over her shoulder at the plastic covered divan and chairs stacked with other bits and pieces on the veran-dah. 'Old place won't know what's happenin'.'

'It's coming together.' Maddy felt an irrational stab of guilt. Irritably she pushed it away. It wasn't her fault that the place no longer belonged to him.

But she couldn't help wondering how it must make him feel to visit now.

'You always move so fast?'

She looked up at him in surprise, suspicious of the implication. 'Why put things off?'

'So you got something to do tomorrow.' Amusement in the blue eyes that matched his shirt.

'Never been my problem.' She shot a glance over his shoulder, distracted. While she appreciated Fraser O'Neill's visit, tradesmen left alone were capable of making serious mistakes.

'Well . . .' she began, 'thanks a lot for letting me know . . .'

Fraser O'Neill took the hint. 'Yeah, better not hold you up then. You've got plenty to do.'

They walked towards the broad front steps, replaced now, secure.

With one foot still on the bottom tread, he turned and squinted up at her in the sunlight. 'You feeling okay now?'

'Great.'

He smiled, nodded, then turned away and slung himself into the pick-up. The long-snouted Shepherd stood panting in the back.

Suddenly Maddy felt as if she might have been rude. He was only being neighbourly, concerned. And people didn't rush the same way in the country. As he started the engine she called out, 'Great looking dog! What's its name?'

'Girlie! But don't tell those women's libbers.' With a grin Fraser O'Neill waved a long arm out of the window and drove away.

CHAPTER FIVE

The inner city restaurant was busy with the sort of cool lunchtime clientele who existed on morsels of exotica served on white platters the size of a car wheel.

Maddy, running late, found her three friends at a table in the shaded courtyard away from the street.

'It was a choice of carbon monoxide poisoning and being seen, or social death and breathing easy,' Rae Bellemore laughed as she accepted a kiss on either cheek. A plump, fun-loving redhead, Rae was married to a wealthy pathologist and long lunches were one of the ways she spent her husband's money. Another was at Maddy's gallery.

Maddy smiled. Not long ago she would rarely have allowed herself time for this sort of protracted interruption to her working day. But she was doing her best to make the changes the doctors had ordered.

Amid warm greetings she pulled up the spare seat between Rae and Jane Corrie. Jane, one of her closest friends, was an editor in a major publishing house and had the too-tense look of a woman three times divorced and 'still looking'. Despite her own hectic schedule she hadn't missed a day visiting Maddy in hospital. Across the table Meg Bennet looked as impeccably groomed as ever, though that hadn't been enough to keep her husband from leaving for another, younger woman. The unexpected bonus however had been extra energy to devote to her computer consultancy – and to ensuring her twin teenage sons turned out nothing like their father.

As a waiter filled Maddy's wine glass, Jane continued her recounting of her latest problems with the opposite sex. '. . . so golf lessons, I thought. That's where you meet men. Aren't they all out there playing sport, working off their testosterone, until some wonderful female rescues them from lonely drunken nights at the clubhouse bar? I buy the gear, the tightest t-shirt I can find, and what the hell do you think happens? I'm stuck in a class with a bunch of women. The damn pro really thought I was there to learn to play golf!'

'Save your dough, Jane.' Meg Bennet lit a defiant cigarette. 'It's a well-known fact that the available, normal, great guy is a figment of the sex-starved female's imagination. They don't exist. Not over thirty-five anyway. After that if they're still single they're neurotic, women haters, or gay.'

'Or all three,' giggled Rae.

Jane shot her a dark look. 'It's all right for you.'

She leaned across the table and spoke in a confiding, slightly slurred whisper. 'Listen, d'you want an earful of heresy? Because this is the most politically incorrect statement you're going to hear this year. I'd like nothing better than to be a kept woman like Rae. I'm sick of being goddamn independent, facing the rat race every day and paying off the mortgage alone. Why did we go and blow it for ourselves? We had it *made*.'

'Hey, hang on, Jane,' Meg put in, 'speak for yourself.' You know the price you pay for that. Control with a capital C. And S for Suppression.'

Rae shook her head of expensive red curls. 'Listen, the only one who ever suppressed me was my mother. After her, Alan was a walkover, believe me.' She turned to Maddy. 'So how's your love life, Maddy? Found the Lone Ranger up there yet?'

'I'm not looking, Rae. Tonto can survive without the Lone Ranger I've found.'

'Come on, Rae, can you imagine Maddy with a cowboy?' Meg raised an incredulous eyebrow.

'Oh, I don't know,' the other woman countered, 'a good-looking hunk with a bit of cow shit on his boots might be perfect.'

Jane Corrie poured herself another glass of wine without waiting for the waiter. 'Oh, sure, someone who thinks Salman Rushdie is Fish-to-go.'

'I didn't actually imply the need to converse, darling.'

Amid the laughter their meals arrived, brought by a twentyish, film-star-handsome waiter well aware of his effect.

He flashed a sunny, perfect smile and exhorted them to 'Enjoy'. With a groan Jane watched the hard, tight discs of his butt as he moved away. 'I don't think I can bear it, knowing I'll never get my hands on a bloke like that again.'

'Darling,' Meg stuck her fork dismissively into a frill of radicchio, 'he's probably got a boyfriend.'

Maddy was the first to leave. As she said her goodbyes, Jane put a hand on her arm. 'I meant to tell you, Maddy . . . I've got tickets to the opening of the Japanese film festival next Friday. Want to join me?'

'Thanks, Jane, but I've finally got the cottage in order. I'm going to try to escape this rat-race most weekends.' She looked around the table. 'Hope I can tempt some of you up for a shot of country air now and then.'

Meg waited until she was out of earshot. 'Can you believe it? Maddy, burying herself in the sticks?'

Rae looked thoughtful. 'It's her health. She's had a scare. Another couple of months and she'll be bored witless. I'll take a bet on it.'

Maddy felt as if she really had managed to get her life more under control.

Forced to take a serious look at her business commitments she saw how she had always expanded her working hours to fill nearly every waking hour.

Dealing with clients, critics, the media, making decisions with accountants and lawyers had been her way of keeping time under control. Of fooling herself there was nothing missing in her life. Frenetic activity in place of love and sexual fulfilment. Like Jane, she supposed. And Meg. Only her body hadn't been able to handle the pace.

Now, in place of dangerous hyperactivity, she had had to learn to delegate, to trust Tony with more of the work she had always handled herself. And there was her retreat to distract her from senseless longing for such unattainable fantasies as love and sex.

She left early Friday afternoon, trying to beat the rush-hour traffic out of the city. By four she was in Wollombi, coming to a stop by the small township's single hardware store.

Eyes followed her as she climbed out of the Saab and made her way up the wide footpath. In a town of four or five hundred, newcomers stood out like a bridesmaid on a honeymoon. Even when they were wearing their oldest pair of jeans.

To Maddy, a hardware store had suddenly become almost as exciting a place to visit as an Armani boutique. She strolled up and down the aisles past the paint and tractor parts, the flyscreen doors, the screws and hammers and nails and bolts.

A new lock for the front door. She'd find someone to put it on. A sturdy torch. A front-door mat. And, her eyes lit up, what she was really looking for – packets of seeds and bags of fertiliser for the vegetable patch she was ready to get into shape.

The friendliness of the service took her aback. A shock to the system after city indifference. She paid for her purchases and the salesman suggested she drive around to the loading dock for the heavy sacks of fertiliser.

'You manage these at the other end okay?'

'Sure.' Somehow she would. Already in her mind's eye she could see the sprouting rows of ferny carrot tops. And there'd be lettuce and tomatoes and beans too. All she needed to do was follow the book she'd been reading and the instructions on the seed packets.

'You the lady's bought the O'Neills' old place?' the middle-aged salesman looked at her with friendly curiosity as he handed back her receipt.

'That's right.' Maddy was sliding her credit card back into her wallet. How the hell had he known?

A big country grin, and her unspoken question was answered. 'Knew by the name on your card. Tom said it was a lady called Tyler.'

Tom Acland. The real estate agent who had sold her the house. Good thing she hadn't told him her bra size. Or when she'd had her last period.

'Hey Del, look! Reckon that's the competition'.

Delmay Bradley stopped what she was doing with the scissors to her caped, dozing client and crossed the salon floor to join her young assistant by the shopfront window.

'Got to be her,' the girl announced. 'Didn't Fraser say she had some fancy black car?'

Del peered through the painted lettering and took in the petite, attractive blonde in too-smart jeans who was stowing her purchases in the back of a dark, expensive looking car. She looked ten years younger and at least a stone or so lighter than Del herself.

'Bit of a sort, Del,' the girl shot her employer a provocative, teasing grin. 'You'd better watch it. She's only spitting distance from Fraser's place.'

The woman had slipped behind the wheel, was backing out, driving off. Del turned away. 'Fraser's not that sort,' she said briskly. 'And anyway he's still getting over Nancy.'

She walked back to her waiting client. 'Stop wasting time, Carol. Mrs J's ready to come out of the dryer.'

But as she resumed her snipping there was a small, persistent frown between Del Bradley's overarched brows. She'd waited a long time for Fraser to get tired of living alone.

Girlie's barking always alerted Fraser when he had visitors. Drying his hands he walked out onto the verandah as the small red sedan came to a stop at the front door.

'Del . . . How are you? Coming in a minute? I was just cleaning up.'

Del smiled brightly as she slammed the door behind her and made her way onto the shade of the verandah. 'You be careful with those sprays Fraser. They're always finding new ones that are dangerous for you.'

He smiled at her concern. 'I'm careful. What you got there?'

'Something for your afternoon tea. Your favourite. I was going to leave it if you weren't around.' Del followed him into the house and put the tea-towel covered plate she was carrying on the kitchen table. She'd made a pretty good guess as to when he'd be back at the house.

'Well, let's have a cuppa together. You got a moment?'

Fraser saw the brightness flicker in Del Bradley's hazel eyes. Del was a good woman, a kind-hearted woman. He cared about her a lot but she could never replace Nancy.

He pulled out a chair and Del took a seat thinking yet again how a woman's touch could really do something with this place. But Fraser wasn't a man you could rush.

He was filling the kettle with water, getting out teapot and cups.

'Saw your new neighbour today.' She kept her eyes on him as she spoke.

Fraser glanced over his shoulder. 'Maddy Tyler?'

'That fancy car isn't going to be much use to her round here.'

A few minutes later Fraser walked over with their tea and sat down across from her. Del saw the amusement in those sky-clear eyes as he pushed the sugar towards her. 'Probably get sick of the place by Christmas.'

Del smiled as she cut Fraser a generous slice of homemade date slice.

After Del left, Fraser set about his usual household chores. Around six he fed Girlie and prepared his own evening meal.

He'd thought of asking Del to stay but still shied away from the implications. It was different when he joined her and a group of her friends at the club on the odd Friday night or for a casual meal in town. But having her alone here with him in the evening might give her the wrong impression.

He didn't want to lead Del on. He liked her company, enjoyed being in a woman's presence, catching a whiff of perfume, noting the sheen on her softly waved reddish hair, watching the way her hips swayed when she walked. Del wasn't young, but she was still attractive. And she knew how to pamper a man, make him feel good about himself.

But for all that, he just wasn't capable of falling passionately in love with her. There wasn't the magic he'd had with Nancy. And when you've had that kind of love you knew better than to settle for anything less.

Anyway, he thought, after almost five years he'd adjusted to his aloneness. God knows how, after almost a quarter of a century of marriage. A slow painful retreat from a shared existence. A sensory withdrawal from the scent, the sound, the feel and taste of the woman he'd loved without reservation.

They'd met in town, standing in line for tickets to the pictures. Something with Ingrid Bergman. Nancy's beautiful smile and dark curly hair had attracted him straight away and they'd hit it off from the beginning. At twenty two, he'd been ready for marriage. And looking.

A farmer's daughter, Nancy had known what it was like to trust your future to the earth and the skies. There'd been good times and bad and she'd worked every bit as hard as he had when she'd had to. He'd seen her fine, girlish skin sucked dry by the sun, felt the callouses on her hands when she'd run them over his nakedness in the dark but nothing could change the way he felt about her. Nancy was special. Calm and serene. Fun and good humoured. Dogged and determined.

But he'd reserved his greatest respect for the strength and resilience she'd displayed when the third of their babies – the one that had finally gone to term – had been lost too.

He'd been the one who'd broken down and wept, wrapped in the strong comfort of arms that should have been cradling their new-born child.

And then, at last, when they had almost given up, there had been Joy.

Every evening when he came back to the house Fraser had felt blessed to be surrounded by the two human beings he loved most in the world. He had felt needed, reaffirmed in his manhood, in his roles as father and husband. He'd had no need for anybody else.

And even when he'd finally lost his fight to keep the farm, had been forced to face the bitter reality of leasing back the home they'd built together, of working his land for someone else, Nancy had never let him feel a failure. Even though it must have pained her just as much she'd helped him come to terms with the bitter loss and blow to his pride. Not so much by what she said but with her quiet understanding of his feelings and needs.

And then, the accident. The storm that had whipped up almost from nowhere when she was out in the back paddock. The tree that had cracked her spine, splintered her ribs into her lungs, left her choking on her own blood. After that he hadn't cared about much any more.

Fraser washed and dried his dinner plate and cutlery. The evenings were still the worst. The television news kept him up to date — but he didn't go much for the other rubbish. At least he'd always liked to read and he had a lot more time these days. Nothing too fancy. A Dick Francis maybe, books that Joy sent him. An occasional visit to the local library.

And then bed. Alone in the room where he and Nancy had given each other so many years of pleasure. There had been a passionate woman behind his wife's quiet smile and they'd taught each other wonderful secrets in the tangle of sweaty sheets.

'You're a fine lover for a farmer, Fraser,' she'd whisper in his ear.

'Not bad yourself for a farmer's wife.' He'd deliver his standard reply. And with muffled happy laughter they'd curl into each other in the darkness.

Now the only sound in the room was the gentle wheeze of Girlie's snoring.

CHAPTER SIX

She took an odd pleasure in the ache of her body. The stiffness affirming her new persona. Maddy. Tiller of the soil.

Oh, God. Giggling, Maddy soaped herself under the brand-new shower head. She had spent most of the day digging and planting her vegetable beds. The sun had been hot on her back, the flies had nipped at her sweat, but the experience had proved immensely satisfying.

When she'd finally come indoors she'd yelped at the sight of herself in the bathroom mirror. Her face and neck were coated with dust except where pale worms of sweat had traced rivulets through the grime. If they could only see me now, she thought in ironic amusement. They – her city friends who were used to seeing her in the expensive urban armour useful for establishing status, sometimes distance, and occasionally envy.

She ran a finger across her filthy cheek. Scratching perhaps to find the real Maddy? She wondered if she'd know her if she found her. And if she was worth finding.

Turning away she began to undress. Funny how coming close to death made you start to think about things. What was important. What wasn't. Whether achievement and success and a revolving door social life were really what it was all about . . .

The shower felt wonderful even despite the faint tackiness of the bore water against her skin. The dirt was skimming off, hurtling into the plughole. She annointed herself with a big dollop of shampoo, lathered up, and suddenly the flow of water ebbed away.

Maddy swore under her breath. Surely not. Not with a head full of shampoo. She fiddled with the taps. Nothing. Dripping, she stepped out of the new shower cabinet and tried the taps above the vanity sink. A gurgle of water then a gasp to nothing.

It was the same in the kitchen. And then Maddy remembered the strange gurglings in the garden hose when she'd done the final watering that afternoon. A sign of things to come – and the timing couldn't have been worse! So what was she going to do? She didn't even have the local phone book. A silly oversight. But, she forgave herself, she hadn't come to the country to be organised. And even if she rang directory, how long would it take to get someone at this time on the weekend?

There was only one thing to do. She wrapped her dripping hair in a towel, slipped on a shirt – no bra – and jeans, and leaving the house unlocked – a deliberate test of faith in her new surroundings – climbed into the Saab.

She could hear the dog barking from inside the house as she came to a stop at Fraser O'Neill's front steps. The door opened and the Shepherd bounded out in front of her owner.

'Girlie. Down. Come here.'

The dog obeyed the low authoritative voice and Maddy opened her car door.

'Mr O'Neill . . . I'm sorry to disturb you . . .'

'It's Fraser to my friends and neighbours. What's up?' He leaned backwards, holding open the screen door. 'D'you want to come in a minute?'

With the dog sniffing at her heels, Maddy followed its owner into the house aware of the incongruous towel wrapped around her wet hair.

For the second time she took a seat in the spartan living area. Needing rescue again.

He nodded when she told him what had happened, smiled when she explained the towel, the shampoo.

'Gardening, eh? Might be you forgot it's not town water around here. Gotta be careful with the stuff.' He delivered the warning gently, but Maddy got the message. City ignorance . . .

Fraser O'Neill went on. 'Tank probably just needs topping up. Either that, or you've sprung a leak in one of the pipes. Some of them're probably due for replacing. Had to do the same myself when Nancy and I first moved in. Hadn't been looked at since Dad built the place.'

Maddy bit her lip. A trickle of very cold water was inching slowly down her neck. 'What do I –?'

Her neighbour stood up. 'I'll come by first thing tomorrow. Might be a problem finding a broken pipe in the dark. And if it's just the tank it'll take a while to fill so I reckon you'd better hop under my shower here' – he saw her expression – 'unless you want to spend all night with that stuff in your hair.'

He found a clean, dry towel – rough and worn – then showed her into the bathroom at the end of the hall. She felt awkward as he stood in the doorway, pointing out the bottle of chain store shampoo on the rim of the large white bath.

'Nothing fancy but it does the trick.'

'Thanks . . . I'll be quick as I can.'

He smiled good humouredly. 'Take your time. There's no one waiting.'

He closed the door and she heard his footsteps moving away, the soft click of the dog's nails following.

The bathroom was spotlessly clean. An old-fashioned polished wood vanity held nothing but a toothbrush and paste in a mug and a bottle of Old Spice.

Maddy couldn't help smiling. No Joop or Fahrenheit or Boss for Fraser O'Neill. Years ago, she remembered, she'd had boyfriends who'd used Old Spice. For one second she felt a crazy impulse to unplug that familiar bottle, to inhale again the scent of girlhood and optimism and boundless expectation . . . But instead she unbuttoned her shirt, feeling a strange, uncomfortable intimacy about stripping off in the house of a man she barely knew.

The overhead lighting was much brighter than she would ever dream of having in her own bathrooms and as she moved to twist on the taps she caught an all too clear glimpse of the soft dimpling on her thighs. Cellulite. The badge of the middle-aged woman.

She looked away. It was one of those things that didn't matter any more. Anyway, who apart from herself, was ever going to see her naked again?

Seven minutes later, damp but thoroughly rinsed hair tucked back into her towel, she was ready to leave. Fraser saw her to her car and this time she had his phone number tucked into the pocket of her jeans.

'Thanks so much. I'm sorry I had to trouble you again.'

'Don't worry about it. Happens all the time. Women stopping by asking to use my shower.'

But Maddy wasn't going to let Fraser O'Neill win them all. Staring out of the open car window into those teasing blue eyes she replied with slow deliberation, 'Maybe you should think about taking down that sign at the front gate.'

A beat. He looked at her. Then a burst of hearty masculine laughter. 'You're right! First thing – next year.' He tapped the car door lightly and stood back. 'Be round tomorrow morning. Eight okay?'

Maddy nodded, waved, and drove off. The faint scent of Old Spice in her nostrils.

'So now you know. Simple. Just got to make sure you keep the tank topped up. Flick this one here.'

Crouched beside him, Maddy nodded as Fraser pointed out the switch under the meter box at the back of the house. She was aware of the denim straining across his broad shoulders.

'Thanks. You can bet your life I won't let that happen again.' Walking side by side they retraced their steps to the front of the house, the dog Fraser's shadow as always.

'You in a hurry? Like a cup of something before you go?' She was eager to get to the vegetable patch again before the sun got too warm but felt compelled to make the neighbourly offer.

'Sounds good to me.'

As he followed her into the house, Fraser found himself thinking how lovely she looked with her fair hair tumbling around her unmade up face. Softer somehow.

He couldn't hide his reaction when he saw what she'd done with the place. The new paint, the expensive looking rugs and furnishings, the ritzy kitchen. He felt the stir of some ambivalent feeling as he took it all in. Remembering how it had been . . . what it had meant to him and to

Nancy . . . Yet he was aware too that despite its makeover the house had not lost its essential character. Maddy Tyler might have tarted the place up but she had known how to keep its soul.

He implied as much as she carried over the tea tray and set it on the wooden table between them.

'You like it?' She poured coffee – plunger, strong, but not as strong as she liked it herself – into the two cups.

'It's . . . pretty. A real womanly feel to it. I reckon Nancy would have loved it.' He took the cup she handed him. Thin china. Expensive he'd bet. It felt awkward in his big fingers.

Maddy leaned back and took a sip of coffee. She looked at the man opposite over the lip of her cup. His tall, lean frame was folded into the blue checked wingback chair.

In the sudden intimacy of the moment it seemed only natural to ask the question. 'You're a widower, Fraser?'

He nodded, then told her briefly about the accident, but even so Maddy caught a glimpse of an emotion she recognised in Fraser O'Neill's eyes. It must have been a good marriage.

'What about you? Married?' It was better than asking if she was, as he suspected, divorced.

'Was. He died too. Long time ago now.' The brisk antiseptic summary. The door slammed quickly on useless emotion.

For a long moment the room was filled with their silence as they sipped their coffee.

Then he said, 'Don't think it'll be too quiet for you around here?'

'That's why I came.'

Fraser O'Neill nodded. One of the reasons anyway, he guessed. Maybe in time he'd find out the rest.

As he was leaving he caught sight of the new lock still in its wrapper on the hall table.

'Needing someone to put that on for you?'

'As a matter of fact, yes. I meant to ask if you knew anyone who might be able to do a bit of work around here.'

'Just let me get some tools out of the pick-up and I'll put it on for you. Won't take a moment.'

'Oh no! Really, Fraser, I don't want to impose any further. Please. If you could just –'

'You need someone – I'm five minutes away. I already told you that.' Ignoring her protestation he strode down the steps, took what he needed out of a metal box fixed to the back of the pick-up and returned to the house.

'Look, Fraser, it's very kind of you, but I can't be obliged. I'm . . . I'm used to being independent. If you insist on doing this then I'm certainly going to pay for your time.'

Busy with a screwdriver he paused to smile up at her. 'Okay, boss, start your stopwatch now.'

They established a pattern of sorts over the next few weekends. On Saturday mornings Maddy would ring with her list of odd jobs and Fraser O'Neill would drop by when he'd finished his other tasks for the day. Afterwards she'd offer him a beer or cold soft drink, pay him their agreed hourly rate and he'd be on his way.

Sometimes, as he drove home, Fraser found himself wondering about his neighbour. At her reserve. At the deliberate distance she kept between them. Oh, she didn't mind talking about her work, could crack a pretty good joke when she wanted to too, but only occasionally did he catch a glimpse of the genuine warmth he suspected lay beneath the careful, controlled exterior. Fraser wondered who had hurt her.

And why she went on hurting herself.

Del Bradley was forced to grit her teeth when her friends and clients found out that Fraser was working for 'that blonde who'd bought his old place'.

'She's working on him, Del. Trying to get her claws in. You know what those types are like. They've got everything but a man.' Reflected in the salon mirrors, their red lips curved in knowing smiles.

'Fraser's not stupid enough to fall for some blatant come-on', countered Del, jabbing a pin into the perming rod with more force than was strictly necessary. 'It's only odd jobs, that's all.'

But while she would have died before admitting it, Del was worried. She'd had her sights set on Fraser O'Neill ever since her divorce became final from the no-good bastard she'd married. She'd been prepared to bide her time, to be patient with a man she knew had truly loved his wife. But sooner or later though she was sure he'd get tired of living alone, would look for the comfort and loving he was used to from a woman.

And Del would be there. She'd made it very clear to every other single woman in town that it was she who'd staked her claim to Fraser O'Neill. Not that that mightn't stop one or two others from trying, but Del knew she could handle them.

But a city woman — younger, slimmer, more attractive . . . Maddy Tyler was a threat she had never envisaged. Surely, she tried to reassure herself, Fraser would have nothing in common with a woman like that? One of those career types who didn't believe in pampering a man, looking after him, and then wondered why they ended up spending their lives alone. As far as Del was concerned, a fancy car and plush apartment could never make up for a man to call your own.

But, her belly clenched, maybe the others were right, maybe Maddy Tyler had come to that conclusion too . . .

She started calling on Fraser more often. Asking as casually as possible about his 'new neighbour'.

'Not so new, Del. Been around a while now. Looks like she really likes the place.' Fraser had his head under the bonnet of the pick-up doing something with the engine.

Del felt a sudden hollowness in her belly. 'You still working round there?'

'Just bits and pieces. Gives me a little extra on the side.'

'What's she like then? Janice down at the pharmacy reckons she's up herself a bit.'

Fraser straightened up, a piece of rubber tubing in his greasy fingers. 'Oh, I wouldn't say that. Quiet more than anything. Keeps herself to herself.'

The dangerous type, Del thought grimly.

CHAPTER SEVEN

'. . . I knew in the first thirty seconds. The moment I saw that vomitous, short-sleeved shirt with the purple and green palm trees. I mean, I'm supposed to flip for a man with all the sartorial style of Sonny Bono circa 1966?'

The wail of a siren in the street outside Maddy's apartment blotted out some of the following details of Jane's latest unsuccessful blind date.

'. . . almost *eight* months, Maddy! Eight months since I've felt a man between my legs. I'm going mad! You know, if they could just find a way to harness all the untapped energy of sex-starved single women the oil and nuclear industries'd be wiped out overnight.'

'I know what you mean,' Maddy murmured into the receiver, at the same time keeping an eye on the usual bloody scenes that were the fodder of the evening television news.

'And you know what gets me *really* mad?' Jane was winding herself up by the moment. 'The bastards know *they're* the ones in demand. *They* call the shots. I mean, doesn't it make you think when even a legend like Lauren Bacall can't get a man?'

'She can *get* a man, Jane. It's a matter of getting the right one.'

'Okay, okay. You know what I mean. The trouble is that now we're all so fabulous it's too damn hard to find someone to match us! It's true, Maddy. I deserve the best. We all do. But you know the old joke about men and car parks – the good ones are taken and the rest are handicapped.'

Maddy thought it time to bring the conversation back to her reason for calling. 'So, about next weekend, Jane. Can you make it?'

There was a pause at the other end of the line. 'Ah . . . just depends if I hear from Carl. He did mention something about Saturday. He's the one with the business in Hong Kong remember? Too short, absolutely no sense of humour, but knows everybody. And has a house at Palm Beach. Can I let you know by Thursday?'

'Maybe we should leave it for another weekend, Jane.' Maddy said goodbye and hung up.

Later, when she was tidying up after her quick solitary meal, Maddy's thoughts went back to that earlier conversation.

Sex. It had been a deep and enduring bond in her marriage to Alex. Progressing from the wild and athletic to a state where the emotional intensity had matched the physical to a degree that had surprised and delighted them both. It was not something she had ever found again with anyone else. The slow melding of body and mind, the complete coma of intense bliss, the tight link of bodies barely moving . . . A totally fulfilling experience unimaginable in any relationship where the heart and body and mind weren't fused.

At first numbed by widowhood, her body gradually came back to life and there'd been times when Maddy had felt as if the blood were overheating in her veins. It shocked her to realise that this was how it must be for men. Aching, driven, obsessed with the need for sexual fulfilment.

And now, after the disappointment of too many inept lovers and with the spectre of AIDS to complicate things even further, she had trained herself not to think about her sexual needs. Celibacy – her unwelcome virtue.

But there were moments when she received unexpected and jolting reminders that she was still a living, breathing sexual being. The odd movie that, unlike *Basic Instinct* or *Fatal Attraction*, offered scenes of genuine eroticism. Or a novel, explicit and sensual in its description of love-making.

Then the long suppressed response would stir inside her. A fluttering in the pit of her belly, a molten desire that heated and fanned out from her thighs. The proof that lust was still alive to taunt her.

And sometimes she would surrender to the only outlet available to her. Would lie in her darkened bedroom, open herself to her own expert caress and quickly and safely explode the grenade of desire. Three, four, or more times.

Never as fulfilling as it had been with Alex but also never as boring or energy-sapping as it might be with an untrained or insensitive lover . . .

And cheaper than a facial, she told herself afterwards when her mirror revealed the new glow on her cheeks.

In the end, her guest list for the weekend was extended to include Jane who, having given up by Thursday on Hong Kong, Too-Short Carl, had called and apologetically requested rescue from a dateless weekend.

Maddy didn't hold a grudge against Jane. Rather she pitied her for failing to take the steps to change her life and develop the resources that would enable her to enjoy her own company.

Yet for a long time after losing Alex she too had been exactly the same. Terrified by the thought of evenings and weekends alone. Desperate for a social life that would fill the empty hours. And in her case, work had been her salvation. Perhaps, she thought dryly, it was not mere ambition that made so many single women rich and successful, but a lack of lovers to distract them with sex and dinners and weekends away.

But having finally learned the importance of balance in her life, Maddy now made time for her own weekends away.

By six on Friday evening her guests had all arrived. Ian Couper and his wife, Diane, were a couple in their late forties, he a well-known sculptor, she a well-hated literary critic. As well there was Anita Lloyd, one of Maddy's most successful artists. A tall, angular woman of thirty-six, she was handsome rather than pretty and did her best work when her love life was complicated. Then there was Jane whose last minute inclusion had relegated her to the smallest bedroom.

Dinner was pleasant. Maddy put together a simple meal of rosemary lamb with salad and they ate at the long wooden table on the verandah.

The air was warm and scented and the conversation flowed as easily as the wine. From art to literature to gossip.

At one stage a particularly satisfying joust developed over Jane's contention that the literati and the critics were continuing to ignore the emergence of popular writing in Australia.

'A bunch of incestuous snobs. That's all you are!' Jane was enjoying herself as she confronted Diane. 'You drink together, screw each other and take turns recommending each other for any grant that's going. On top of that you're petrified to give a mate a bad review in case he might do the same to your next book.'

'What's wrong, Jane?' Diane Couper gave her a meaningful smile. 'Piers Sullivan knock you back?'

'Listen, sweetie, Piers only sleeps with his current editor or anyone on the Grants committee – either sex, it doesn't matter.'

'Getting back to the main argument,' said Maddy quickly, 'why the cringe about anything that reaches a popular market? It's not only books either, it's art too. Yet we don't seem to mind braying about the success of films like *Muriel's Wedding* or *Strictly Ballroom*.'

Jane snorted. 'The literati hate anyone who can turn a non-government buck from writing. It's a threat to the whole handout system.'

'Oh, let's be fair,' Anita interjected. 'It's not only the local successes they cannibalise – look what they did to Erica's menopausal tome. Without exception every single review I've read that was written by a female was a bitchy put-down of Jong. Whatever happened to the sisterhood?'

'I'll tell you what happened,' Jane's eyes were brilliantly aglow. 'They've never forgiven Erica for getting more than them. More sex, more money, more acclaim.'

'She'd scare the life out of most men.' Ian Couper offered his in-depth male point of view. He had the flushed contented look of a man four drinks ahead of his wife.

'You see!' Jane was moved enough to release the stranglehold on her wine glass and stab a triumphant finger on the tabletop. 'Men can't cope with strong, independent women! They'd love us all to be meek, submissive and completely under their control. They can't handle being involved with a woman who's in charge of her own life.'

Diane Couper shook her head and said firmly. 'Things are changing, Jane. And anyway look at Ian — he's never been like that.'

Maddy suppressed a smile as she stood to clear the plates. She could guess exactly what Jane was thinking. That Ian Couper was a wimp, dominated by his bombastic, controlling wife. Definitely not the sort of man that Jane would ever be attracted to.

Yet she hated the other type too . . .

It was all too complicated, Maddy thought. She was glad to be out of the race.

The next morning while Jane and the Coupers set off on a tour of the local vineyards Anita joined Maddy for coffee on the verandah.

'How do you cope without the Saturday newspapers?' she looked wonderingly at Maddy.

'A marvellous habit to rid oneself of,' Maddy responded. 'No critics to affect my blood pressure, no guilt about the death and destruction in the rest of the world, no nightmares about the deficit, le Bombe, or Yeltsin's drinking problem.'

Anita chose a slice of wholemeal toast from the covered basket. Her long straight hair swung over a strong-featured face devoid of make-up. 'Maybe you're right, Maddy. I can see what this place has done to you. You're calmer, more relaxed. I think it was exactly what you needed.'

'It took a while — and one hell of a shock — but I see that now.'

Anita stopped buttering her toast and looked up. 'You know, maybe I shouldn't say this, but, well, I always felt you were looking for . . . something more.'

From behind her dark glasses Maddy looked out over the harsh beauty of the surrounding countryside. After a very long moment she said quietly, 'Maybe I've found it.'

The others returned in time for lunch and again the meal was taken outside.

'More visitors, darling.' Helping herself to another slice of ham, Jane drew attention to the approaching pick-up. 'Better open another bottle.'

Maddy was on her feet. 'It's my neighbour. He does a few odd-jobs for me when I need him.'

Diane had been lolling booze-languid in her chair. Suddenly alert she turned to Maddy in gleeful confrontation. 'Don't tell me some *bloke's* the reason you buried yourself up here, Maddy! Now why didn't I work that one out!'

Not bothering to reply, Maddy walked out into the sunshine to greet Fraser. But a flush of irritation heated her cheeks. She hoped her neighbour hadn't heard that slurred, ringing voice.

'G'day, Maddy.' Fraser slammed the truck door and lifted his hat in the courtly, old-fashioned greeting she'd grown used to. 'You want me to do something about that side fence, right?' Girlie was panting by his heels.

'A couple of those posts look like they need replacing, Fraser.' Maddy felt suddenly awkward. She hadn't given any thought to this particular moment. What did she do now? Introduce Fraser to the others? Ask him to join them for a drink? If she didn't, would he think she didn't feel him worthy of meeting her friends?

But then she thought of Diane. Something made her want to protect Fraser from that sort of brittleness.

'Uh . . . I'd ask you to join us, Fraser, but we're just clearing up. Maybe later, when you've finished . . .' She trailed off.

'Thanks, but I'd better get started here. Gotta take all that wire out if I'm going to do it properly. Then I'd better dash. Got things to do in town later.'

His blue eyes smiled into hers before he turned away and Maddy knew he was saving both of them any awkwardness.

'Maddy, my sweet, your little secret is exposed! Aren't you going to ask him up for a drink? I want to see that rugged handsomeness up close.'

'Can it, Diane. The guy *works* for me I told you.'

'But a neighbour, you said.' Jane had joined the game. 'And look at that body. That's *not* City Central gym. It's honest, hard work. Don't you just love that in a man? Go for it Maddy! I would.'

As Fraser walked away Maddy could only hope he was out of earshot.

'Change to see Levis outside the latest Oyster Bar or Coke commercial, isn't it Jane?' Anita was studying Maddy's neighbour through her Ray Bans. 'Looks like the strong, silent type to me.'

Diane Couper giggled. 'See, Maddy, you wouldn't even have to talk to him. No conversations about Brett Easton Ellis, Dadaism or Tarentino. Just silent, unadulterated lust.'

'Come on girls!' It was her husband's turn to chime in. 'Maddy's not desperate enough to hump some country hick.'

Maddy stood up, a dirty plate in each hand. 'I'm washing up and one of you lazy sods is helping me.'

She disappeared into the house.

Filled with a sense of overwhelming relief Maddy pulled back the covers and slipped between the fine printed sheets. The others had left and the house was peaceful, still. Hers again.

The grandfather clock in the hall ticked steadily in accompaniment to her quiet contemplation. Something had happened to her that day. She'd found herself angered and shocked by her friends' smart-mouthed quips. It was as if their cutting banter had somehow belittled – *contaminated* was the word that sprang into her mind – this haven she had found for herself. And the people in it.

Maddy realised she had already made her decision. From now on she would keep her two worlds totally separate. Would allow no over-lapping. Her entertaining would be done in the city, and the cottage would remain her very private retreat.

Because she now knew that what she had found here was too precious to share with anyone else.

CHAPTER EIGHT

There was the usual line waiting for service in the bank and Fraser chatted patiently with the customer behind him. He'd known George Halligan's boy since he was a baby, and the two of them discussed the sorts of topics that are always newsworthy to those who make their living from the land: the weather, fertiliser, feed and fuel prices, expected yields.

Then it was Fraser's turn to be attended to. As he completed his business with the teller he felt a tap on his shoulder.

'Oh, g'day, Bob.' Fraser smiled. 'How're things?'

Bob Carmody, a big-bellied, florid-faced man a couple of years older than Fraser had just emerged from the manager's office. He owned a spread on the other side of town and was a big wheel in the local Chamber of Commerce.

'Paying in those special cheques are you, Fras?' There was a suggestive smile on the other man's red, fleshy face. He gave Fraser a wink. 'They tell me she's a real looker.'

Fraser had wondered how long it would take before the drumbeat of gossip got around. He gave the fat man an easy smile. 'The way I see it, Bob, the lady's not looking and neither am I.' Thanking the teller, Fraser accompanied Bob Carmody to the exit. The line of customers hadn't shortened by much. 'By the way, Bob,' Fraser's voice was a little louder than usual, 'you ever get to the bottom of that little problem you had with the Chamber's accounts?'

Maddy's life had changed. She didn't bother with excuses to herself any longer when she left the city so much earlier.

Often she would head for the cottage on Thursday evening, returning either late Monday or early Tuesday morning. It was something she could do now that she had allowed Tony to take more responsibility at the gallery. He was clearly enjoying his expanded role and Maddy wished she'd learned the value of delegating a long time ago.

Other things had changed too. The hectic social life that had once spun her around the city's fashionable nightspots and parties now held little appeal. Increasingly, the only invitations she found herself accepting were those from her very closest friends. For it hadn't taken her long to see that the time she spent at the cottage gave her something special. The moment she opened the door and entered that quiet, welcoming space, a sense of peace crept through her bones. Everything that sustained her was there.

The only person she saw on those long week-ends was Fraser O'Neill and gradually she began to admit that she looked forward to his company. It gave her pleasure to be in the house and hear the faint sound of his tractor slashing one of the paddocks, to see him in the distance bringing to life the couple of acres of vines that had been unattended for so long, to listen to his whistle from the top of a ladder as he cleaned leaves out of the cottage gutters.

She even found herself prolonging the time they spent together when Fraser had finished with his chores. As dusk fell they would sit over drinks on the verandah and Maddy would encourage him to fill her in on the history of the area, about how Wollombi Brook had also been known as Cock Fighter River after the ritual that had taken place there during the convict days, about the families who could trace their ownership of the land back a hundred years. And she learned a little too about dairying and winemaking, harvests and droughts. Desultory conversation. Nothing personal. Never intrusive or demanding.

Fraser had not failed to notice the changes in his neighbour. He enjoyed their chats and had seen Maddy Tyler start to relax. The reserve was still there but he sensed that the tension was gradually ebbing away. She had grown calmer, softer, more down to earth and as the brittle veneer slowly peeled away Fraser got glimpses of the warm and vulnerable woman that lay beneath. He noticed too how she would fondle Girlie's head and stroke the thick, wolf coat as she listened to him talk. The repetitive, gentle gesture seemed to do as much to soothe Maddy Tyler as it did the animal by her side.

'She likes you,' he said once when Maddy was stretched out on the top step with Girlie's head on her lap.

Maddy smiled. 'She's a one-man dog.'

'You're right. My daughter gave her to me after her mother died. Said I needed company. A real house dog. Not those working dogs we'd always had when we ran the cattle.'

'The pups must be due any day.' Maddy ran gentle fingers over the dog's distended belly. He had told her he wanted Girlie to have a final litter. Would keep a pup for himself and give the rest away.

'Yeah, I'll be up all night supervising the feeds.' She laughed.

And Fraser O'Neill liked the sound. Almost as much as he liked Maddy Tyler.

It was a Saturday morning and Maddy made the short trip into town for the paint Fraser would require later that day. By now the male staff in the hardware store greeted her like an old friend. As the purchase was added to her account the store manager grinned. 'You're makin' sure my kids get a college education, Maddy.'

She made some joking reply but as she turned to go Maddy felt warmed by a growing sense of acceptance and belonging. A rare experience for someone raised on city anonymity and indifference.

Storing the paint tin in the boot of her car, she crossed the road to the supermarket. She was on her way back to the Saab when she remembered. Damn. Shampoo. But she wasn't going back to stand in that supermarket line-up again. No one hurried in the country, she'd come to realise. Not when there was conversation and gossip to exchange. With a frown she looked along the street. Wasn't there a salon . . .?

She spotted the sign and it was just two doors up from where she had parked.

The ping of the doorbell announced her entry and heads swivelled to check out the new arrival. At least four pairs of eyes grew wider.

Maddy waited at the counter as a middle-aged woman with tinted red hair put down her scissors and comb and moved towards her.

'Good morning.' It was Del's first close-up look at Maddy Tyler and she was making the most of it. 'Can I help you with something?' Del could hardly believe her luck.

Maddy's eyes were searching the display rack of hair care products. 'Just a shampoo, thank you. Anything.'

'Best to get something for your hair type. Normal? Dry?' A beat . . . 'Coloured?'

A faint titter came from the back of the room.

'This'll do fine, thank you.' Maddy selected a plastic bottle from the stack.

The woman took her money and dropped the purchase in a red plastic bag with gold lettering. As she handed it over she asked, 'Excuse me, but you're Maddy Tyler, aren't you? The gallery owner from Sydney?'

Del felt gratified by Maddy's look of surprise. She always read the Sydney Sunday papers, especially the gossip and social pages. She hadn't missed the piece that went: 'Seems that Maddy Tyler, high-flying owner of the Tyler Gallery, is serious about changing her lifestyle. Swapping the power suits and black lace for moleskins and boots, she now disappears most weekends to her newly acquired country retreat . . .'

Maddy nodded in reply to Del's question. 'That's right.'

'I'm Del Bradley, Maddy. I own the salon here and I was actually intending to get in touch with you.' Del had worked out her plan and Maddy's unexpected appearance had made things easier. 'You see, I knew the minute I read you were in the art business that you'd be absolutely perfect.'

'I'm sorry?' Maddy was confused. She had no idea what the woman was talking about.

So Del explained. About the Art Show at the Community Hall. The proceeds to go to the Rural Fire Brigade. 'I'm the president of the organising committee and I was hoping you might be kind enough to judge the entries for us. It's such a good cause and we'd be ever so grateful.'

Maddy took a closer look at the woman smiling expectantly at her across the counter. She was smartly dressed in a two-piece cream suit, her make-up perfect, gold at her ears and throat.

'Well . . . I . . .'

A country art show. But Maddy saw she was being offered another chance for inclusion, acceptance.

As Del gave her dates and times, Maddy could just imagine what they would think back in Sydney . . .

'I'd better not hang around today, Maddy. Now that I'm a father, I mean.' Fraser spoke over his shoulder as he packed his tools and bits and pieces into the pick-up.

Girlie had given birth a few days before. Five pups – three male, two female. Fraser had found homes for all of them except the one he intended keeping for himself but they wouldn't be ready to leave their mother for a few more weeks.

As she watched him get ready to leave Maddy felt a sudden stab of disappointment that surprised her. She realised she'd grown used to the hour or so she and Fraser spent together after he'd finished work.

'I had a look at that roof. Think you're going to have to replace some of those panels before the wet arrives.'

'Okay. Just tell me what I have to get.' From where she stood on the verandah Maddy saw Fraser hauling something out from under the tarpaulin cover in the back of the pick-up. He lifted it over the edge and carried it up to her.

'Thought you might do with this. Used to belong to the house. Didn't ever fit our new place.'

Maddy saw it was a beautiful, intricately wrought firescreen.

'Oh, Fraser, it's lovely! I was going to try and find one in Sydney before winter. But –'

'Now you can save yourself the bother. I'll take it inside for you.'

'But –' Maddy followed him into the house, 'I can't just let you *give* me this, Fraser. Please. You must let me pay you what it's worth.'

For a moment Fraser made no reply. He had other things to think about as he placed the screen where it had been when he and Nancy lived in this house.

Then he turned to look at the woman next to him. The woman whose guard, even now, sometimes seemed every bit as impenetrable as the metal screen that stood back in its rightful place.

'You know, Maddy,' he said quietly, his blue eyes holding hers, 'everything doesn't have to come with a price.'

Those softly spoken words hung in the air long after Fraser O'Neill had gone and left her alone.

What's happened to me? Maddy brooded as she sat in the quiet house. A simple gesture of friendship and she had almost spoilt it. Had tried to insist on making it a financial transaction. When, she wondered, had she become the sort of person who judged everything in monetary terms? Who expected nothing without obligation?

Yet she could remember a time when she had understood the pleasures of giving. When she was younger she'd been open and generous and warm. When had she become so defensive, so out of balance with herself?

After Alex died, she thought. Then everything changed. Losing belief in emotional security she'd replaced it with security of another kind. Money protected her, became her defence, made her reliant on no one. Ah, yes, Maddy Tyler had achieved that pinnacle of fulfilment – self-sufficiency.

So that a simple gesture of goodwill became a dizzying threat.

The following Saturday morning Maddy drove into town to fulfil her role as judge of the fundraising art show. She was met by a smiling Del and three other committee members on the front steps of the community centre, a soulless brick tribute to local government design.

Del introduced the others – 'Please, it's Maddy' – and escorted her into the hall where the various entries were displayed on hessian clad walls.

'It's very good of you to do this for us, Maddy. We really couldn't have got anyone better.' It didn't cost Del anything to reiterate her appreciation. She presented Maddy with a catalogue and pointed out the various categories of entry. 'Now, what do you think? Is it best we just leave you to get on with it?'

'I think so. I'll let you know when I'm ready.'

It took Maddy close to three hours to make an accurate assessment of the winners. And though she'd expected to be less than impressed, she was very pleasantly surprised. A number of the winning entries showed quite outstanding talent. By the time Del reappeared at her side, Maddy had completed her list of entries worthy of a prize.

'You've got some real talent here. I wouldn't be ashamed to have a couple of these painters represented in my own gallery.'

'*Well,*' Del raised an appreciative eyebrow, 'that's a real compliment.'

'In fact,' Maddy was making a note against the catalogue, 'if it's not too late I'd like to donate a cash prize to the most outstanding entry.'

Del opened her eyes in surprise. Well, whatever next . . .

The evening went without a hitch. Maddy's generous last-minute gesture was loudly acclaimed and later, at supper, she sat with Del Bradley and the full complement of her ladies' committee.

The women were friendly but Maddy could sense they were summing her up. But then, she reminded herself, women were always harder to win over than men.

CHAPTER NINE

Del brought her small red sedan to a stop outside the cottage door. There had been little opportunity to pursue her cause at last night's supper. Today would be different.

The woman she'd come to see had appeared at the front door. 'Oh . . . Del. How are you?' It was a warm morning and Maddy was dressed in a long, loose fitting, off-white dress. She had a mug of something in her hand.

Del smiled as she climbed the stairs and proffered the cellophane-wrapped bouquet of mixed flowers. 'The ladies asked me to pass on their thanks. We're all very grateful for your efforts in helping us. And the artist's over the moon about her prize money.'

'Oh . . .' Maddy was touched by the gesture. 'Well, thank you. It was my pleasure.' Accepting the flowers from Del's hands, she stood back with an inviting gesture. 'Come in for a moment. Would you like a cup of coffee? Tea?'

'Something cold would be lovely.' As she followed Maddy inside the house, Del's hazel eyes swept over the furnishings, the expensive rugs on the newly polished floors, the array of interesting knick-knacks and the paintings on the walls.

'Well . . . if you don't mind me saying so, haven't you done a lot with this.' It was impressive Del Bradley told herself, if a little overdone.

Maddy looked surprised as she opened a kitchen cupboard and found a glazed brown jug for the flowers. 'You knew the place before?'

'Yes, when Fraser and Nancy lived here, before it was sold to Jim Lancaster.' She looked around, one eyebrow raised. 'Takes money of course.'

'You knew Fraser's wife?' Maddy poured two glasses of orange juice, handed one to her unexpected visitor, and gestured at the wingback chairs.

Del sat, carefully crossing her legs to best effect.'Oh, yes, Nancy and I were very good friends. Very,' she emphasised. 'In fact I'm on my way to Fraser's now. He loves my date slices. I bake him one every week. Poor man needs looking after now that he's on his own.'

Her eyes were fixed on the woman opposite, searching for a reaction.

'He must miss his wife a lot.'

Del shot her a sharp look. 'Nancy was everything to that man. He'll never let anyone take her place.'

'That comes across loud and clear.'

Del drove it further. 'The sort of love those two had comes only once in a lifetime.'

'I know. That's how it was for me too. Only I never had the joy of all the years Fraser had.'

Del hid her surprise. Maddy Tyler certainly hadn't struck her as the sort of woman who'd speak quite so personally to a stranger. But since that particular door had been opened . . . 'Do you mind my asking how . . .?'

'Leukemia. We had six years together. Four of them married.'

'I'm sorry. It must have been terrible for you.' A beat. Then she went in again. 'And now . . .? There's no one else?'

Maddy shook her head with a gentle smile. 'No. And there isn't going to be.' The simple assertion of fact that had taken so many years of pain and emptiness and vain searching to evolve.

Mission accomplished, a short time later Del rose to go. She felt assured there was no threat here. From either party.

But then, as she walked with Maddy down the hall her eye caught something that rocked her newly found reassurance.

'Goodness.' Stopping in her tracks Del stared through the open door into the living room. 'That screen. It's Fraser's isn't it?'

'Yes.' Maddy had picked up something odd in Del's tone. 'He insisted I have it. Said it was made especially for the house. And it is lovely, isn't it?'

Del nodded, then said slowly, 'It was Fraser's housewarming gift to Nancy all those years ago.'

Later, as she thought back on the conversation with her unexpected visitor Maddy couldn't believe she had spoken as openly as she had. Why in the world had she confided, no matter how fleetingly, in a woman she barely knew?

What was it about this place, these people, that she had suddenly felt the need to unpick the tight stitches of the past?

Or, she wondered, had some fundamental change taken place in herself?

It happened two weeks before Christmas. A day that started like any other. Fraser had come and worked on the roof, doing his best to replace the suspect sheets of tin before the hoped-for seasonal rains. Now he was packing up to leave.

'If it's all right with you I'll drop by first thing tomorrow morning, Maddy. I don't want to leave that tarp on a moment longer than I have to.'

Usually a couple of hours were enough for Fraser to finish the few tasks. But replacing sections of the aging corrugated roof was a bigger job and one that couldn't be done in stages.

'Sure. No problem.'

'See you tomorrow then.' He was opening the door of the pick-up.

And it was then she heard herself say, 'Like to stay for lunch tomorrow when you're through?'

He turned to look at her. A moment's hesitation, then a smile and nod. 'Sounds good to me.' And a teasing light in those deep blue eyes. 'Doesn't mean I have to get toffed up, does it?'

By six-fifteen that same evening Fraser had already eaten and was standing outside frowning up at the prematurely darkening sky. Amid deep grunts of thunder and bright quivers of lightning huge mountains of clouds were rolling in from the west. It was the green tinge to them that had him worried.

On top of that a low, mean, howling wind had joined the stage show in the last twenty minutes or so and his hair was now whipping around his upturned face.

Fraser knew the signs like a doctor knows a disease. They didn't happen often, but when they did these sharp sudden summer storms could strike with dangerous ferocity. And he had learned the hard way to respect nature's violent deceit.

He returned to the house, closed everything up, then locked a nervous Girlie in the laundry with the remaining pup he was keeping.

As he passed by the telephone he thought about ringing but figured there was a hell of a lot of electricity around. And he knew he didn't have a moment to lose.

By the time he arrived at the cottage the wind had grown even stronger and the flashes of lightning more frequent. It was clear she hadn't heard the pick-up arrive and he had to hammer at the door with his fist. As he waited, he could hear the wild flapping of the tarp on the roof.

'Who is it?' City caution. Fraser could hear the nervous note in her voice but wasn't sure if it was due to an unexpected evening visitor or the approaching storm.

'It's me, Maddy, Fraser!'

She struggled to open the door against the wind and he saw her worried face. 'Oh, Fraser, I —'

'Close everything up. I think we're in for it, but it won't last long. I'm going to fix that tarp more securely. Dig out the candles if you've got any.'

Before she could reply he was running for the shed to get the ladder.

He did the best he could and had only just made it back inside before the storm hit with a vengeance.

'Oh, God . . .' Maddy had never experienced anything like it. And certainly never in an old timber cottage. The place shook and trembled as the rain lashed down and the wind roared and howled like a demon. Within minutes the lights in the kitchen flickered and were gone.

She found an old hurricane lamp and as Fraser lit a match its weak light showed him the fear in her face.

'It'll be okay.' He had to put his mouth close to her ear to make himself heard and was accosted by the faint scent of flowers wafting from her neck and hair.

Then — a cannon roar of noise, white light whipping around the room as the full force of nature's weaponry was unleashed.

She jumped, instinctively moving closer, and in an unselfconscious instant response his arm went protectively around her shoulders.

'It won't last long, I promise.' For some reason his voice wasn't his own. It was something to do with the shock of contact with the remembered softness of the female form.

Maddy too was conscious of the unexpected intimacy. She was close enough to breathe in Fraser O'Neill's clean, male scent and feel the lines of his long, lean body. There was a strangeness and familiarity at the same time at once more being in a man's embrace.

'Oh *God*!' To Maddy, it sounded as if the lightning had scored a direct hit on the roof. Trembling, she clutched at Fraser's shirt and he drew her closer against his chest.

And suddenly there was an unsteadiness to her breathing. Her heart was banging against her ribs and she knew it was more than fear. Wrapped in the comfort of Fraser's arms, she felt the tension flow out of her body. She had almost forgotten this sense of warmth and security. And it was then, in the middle of that raging storm, that she acknowledged her growing attraction to Fraser O'Neill and realised he was one of those rare men – the sort who offered the quiet strength and presence that made a woman feel safe.

Even a woman who had grown used to looking after herself.

'It's moving on.' The words were warm against her ear and Maddy quivered as she felt his hand begin to stroke her spine. Stirred and confused, she lifted her head and in the flickering half-light their eyes met and held.

And then, above the drumming of the rain and the crack of lightning, the shrill ringing of the telephone blew the moment away. Startled, Maddy broke away from his hold and reached for the receiver but felt Fraser's quick warning touch on her bare arm. 'Let it be, Maddy. It's dangerous in a storm.'

She looked at him, the moment of intimacy shattered. And then she nodded. He was right. It was dangerous.

Like so much in life.

Two hours or so later when Maddy went to bed power had still not been restored. As soon as the storm had passed Fraser, reassuring himself that the tarpaulin cover had held, left her alone. He'd promised to return first thing in the morning.

As she undressed in the flickering lamp light Maddy thought back to what had happened in the kitchen earlier that evening. She remembered how she'd felt when Fraser O'Neill had held her, the stirring in her body, how much she had enjoyed it. The embers of her dormant desire had flickered into life and for a few moments her body had taunted her with the old familiar longings.

It was still there, she admitted to herself as she slipped between the sheets. The hunger. Sexual desire doesn't go away, it just waits to ambush you. At the craziest of times.

Extinguishing the lamp she lay in the darkness and indulged herself in an emotionally charged replay of the scene with Fraser. She had known by the expression in his eyes, the touch of his hands that he had felt it too. Which came as no real surprise. For the way she'd read the picture, Fraser had been missing out for a long time too.

So, she asked herself, what was she going to do about it? The idea of sleeping with Fraser O'Neill was appealing. She was attracted to his lean, hard body and the warmth in those sexy, blue eyes. He made her laugh, his dry laconic humour still capable of catching her unawares. But there was an inner strength too. She'd learned that over the last few months. Integrity and sincerity. The quiet confidence of a man with nothing to prove. A man at peace with himself. And Maddy sensed it had something to do with his connection to the land. In a way she was just beginning to understand for herself, nature restored him. So what happens next? Start an affair? Ease the longing in her blood? At least, the pragmatic thought struck her, she could be sure that Fraser wasn't gay, bisexual, a drug user.

Maddy closed her eyes and allowed herself to develop the fantasy of what might have happened if that telephone hadn't rung when it did. Then she told herself she was crazy.

In his own dark bedroom Fraser O'Neill wasn't doing any better a job of ignoring what had occurred. Until the moment when he had taken Maddy Tyler in his arms he hadn't understood that contentment is rarely a static state.

For so long he'd been sure he was content with his single existence. Told himself he'd got used to doing without a woman. Until tonight. When he realised how much he'd been missing.

Now contentment had been replaced by confusion and the heat of sexual longing.

Tossing restlessly on the wide vacancy of his bed Fraser recalled the soft contours of her body, the hypnotic scent of her hair and skin, and now, as then, felt flooded with desire. A sensation that both delighted and mortified him.

He'd get over it, he told himself firmly. It was just that he'd been without a woman for so long. A natural response. Nothing would come of it.

He wasn't that much of a fool.

The power had come on sometime during the night and she was preparing breakfast when she heard him arrive.

Maddy pushed open the screen door and called out a greeting. 'Hi. I've just made coffee. Would you like some?'

'Thanks, but I'd better get started. Might take me longer if there's been more damage up there.'

There was nothing different in his tone of voice yet Maddy wondered if he was avoiding her eye as he busied himself with pulling what he needed out of the truck.

'Well, give me a call if you change your mind.'

He looked at her then and she felt relieved to see no awkwardness in his smile. 'Sure.'

At twelve, just as she was thinking about lunch, he tapped on the door. 'I'm going to need some extra bolts and rivets and there's another couple of sheets the wind got to that need replacing. That okay?'

'Of course. Would it help if I went into town?'

'Thanks,' he looked hot under the brim of his hat, 'but I'll need the truck to load the sheets.'

'What about lunch? Do you –'

He shook his head. 'No . . . thanks, but there's still a lot to do. I'll grab a sandwich in town and eat it on the way back.'

As she watched him drive off she couldn't tell if he was finding an excuse to avoid her company.

She smiled to herself as she walked back into the house. Fraser O'Neill hadn't struck her as shy.

It was already dusk by the time he'd finished. She waited until he'd packed his truck and then invited him in for a cold beer. She never drank it herself but had taken to keeping a supply in the fridge for him.

As Fraser lifted his glass Maddy found herself noticing the tiny scar above his top lip, the slim, strong fingers, the way his in-need-of-a-cut hair curled over his collar.

The glass was almost empty when she said, 'I've made enough dinner for both of us, Fraser. Can you stay?' She hated the way her heart trampolined as she waited for his reply.

There was a long beat. Then he gestured to his stained and rumpled work shirt. 'Like this? I'm –'

'No problem,' she cut in, then doused her too speedy response with an attempt at humour. 'This isn't Betty Windsor's. The bathroom's all yours. I owe you a return visit.'

But he chose instead to wash in the laundry off the kitchen, shirt rolled down to his waist, leaning over the tub to splash off the dirt.

From where she stood at the stove Maddy had a clear view of Fraser O'Neill's bare, tanned back. Strong and muscular. No spare flesh. Wide shoulders tapering down to narrow hips. From the rear, she thought, he looked like a man twenty years younger. And the effect was strangely unsettling.

He was drying himself now, rubbing the towel briskly over back, shoulders, face. 'Oh, God . . .' Sounding aggrieved, he looked down at the towel. 'I'm sorry, Maddy. You shouldn't have given me this.'

'What is it?' Leaving the simmering pot on the stove she walked over to where he stood at the tub.

'Must've cut my face. Got blood on your white towel.'

Peering forward, she looked at his face. 'It'll come off. Let me see what you've done.'

A thin cut ran from his temple to his ear. 'Looks like the metal got you. Wait a sec.'

As he leaned over the sink she went to fetch cotton wool, antiseptic, a packet of bandaids.

'Just stick something on it,' he demurred, 'so I don't make a mess.'

Taking no notice of his request, Maddy pointed to the wooden chair beside the tub. 'Sit down so I can reach you.'

He did as he was told and, with her face hovering close to his, she began to dab at the cut with the antiseptic.

Breathlessly aware of his bare torso . . . Of those quiet blue eyes looking back into her own . . . And her fingers were unsteady as she opened a bandaid and stuck it over the wound.

'There.'

The catch in that one word told him everything he needed to know. His hand found hers and gripped it tightly. Their eyes stayed locked as he stood up and encircled her waist and Maddy shuddered at the touch of his naked chest. Then he was leaning down to kiss her. And she kissed back. A long, soft shiver of a kiss that made breathing an irrelevancy.

And when they'd kissed and kissed again, the dream they'd both entered took them to her bedroom where they threw off their clothes and lay beside each other in uninhibited nakedness.

Their lovemaking was a slow spiral dance, a drumbeat of passion. His mouth and hands made secret and exciting trails across her breasts and belly and thighs. He licked and kissed her lips, her eyes, her ears with a confidence and skill that thrilled her. His masculine power was unassailable yet she felt neither engulfed nor diminished. Fraser O'Neill was strong and capable and practised. He knew about gentleness and rhythm and timing.

And when he could tell she was ready he moved inside her, and it was then Maddy made the breathless discovery that she was with a man who understood about tenderness, about sexual fulfilment being a journey of the mind as well as the flesh.

And with a moan of greedy pleasure she yielded. Trusted him to take her to an ocean far away where he drowned them both in the waves of total and tumultuous union.

CHAPTER TEN

Maddy felt like a long-term prisoner who'd suddenly been released without notice.

The fact that she'd ended up in bed with Fraser was startling enough. Yet it was the sheer intensity of their sexual encounter that really stunned her.

She remembered the teasing comments of Jane and the others when they'd first seen Fraser O'Neill. Had they observed before she had, the sensuality that lay beneath that quiet, laconic manner? She, who had always been intrigued by the cobra of sexuality that can lie coiled and hidden beneath the most civilised of masks.

Images of that night of lovemaking filled her belly and throat with warm flutterings. She remembered how it had felt to be sucked into that whirlpool of erotic sensation. And afterwards, beached in his arms, she had found a different sort of pleasure. Comfort. Warmth. Peace.

Later, in the thin light of dawn he'd slipped out of bed and she'd watched him dress in the half light. When he was ready he bent over and kissed her cheek. 'I'm not sure if you know it, Maddy, but you've given me something very, very special.'

From beneath the covers she reached out for his hand and answered softly, her voice drugged with pleasure. 'You were pretty generous yourself.'

He squeezed her hand. 'I'll let you get some sleep.'

Then, just before he closed the bedroom door she said in a soft, sleepy voice, 'I'm usually here by six, Fridays, Fraser.'

'I'll be here.'

She listened until the sound of the pick-up died away.

There was plenty to keep her busy the following week and for that Maddy was glad. She had to finish planning the gallery's program for the year ahead and then there was the usual burgeoning social agenda as December approached. Yet no invitation was important enough to keep her from the cottage the following weekend.

As she headed out of the city on Friday afternoon she felt the sharp daggers of anticipation in her body, the dancing of her nerve ends at what was to come. The sexual encounter with Fraser had caught her completely unawares but the idea of a weekend lover now seemed the perfect way of appeasing the newly aroused gods of desire.

It was good to share intimacy with someone she *liked* so much, someone she felt comfortable with and physically excited by. To share a wonderful erotic experience without demands or expectations. She and Fraser were two people with completely different working lives who needed no more from each other than warmth and physical contact, release for their very normal human desires.

It was the perfect answer for both of them.

Fraser had been watching the clock since four. When six o'clock finally arrived he gave her half an hour and then finally couldn't bear to wait a moment longer.

His heart was flipping crazily as he pulled up at the cottage. He had forgotten what it felt like to have feelings like this.

She was watching for him and opened the door before he had time to knock, looking lovely in a pair of slim fitting navy pants and a pale pink shirt.

'Maddy . . .' But she didn't need words any more than he did. He took her in his arms and felt hers go around his waist. With a smile she turned her face up to his and he gave a long shuddering breath and then they were kissing. The sorts of kisses Fraser had dreamed of in the days in between. The sorts of kisses that exploded something inside his veins.

In the bedroom they danced the same naked dance and once more their steps led them to that place of exhausted, dizzy delight.

And later, as before, he left before the dawn.

Body still languid from the night before, Maddy stood at the kitchen window and sipped at her coffee. In the far paddock she could see the moving blue spot of Fraser's denim shirt and her eyes lit with wry amusement. She still found it hard to believe that the man in the distance atop the tractor had become her lover.

A tractor, for God's sake. Faded jeans and rough workman's hands . . . She, who was used to slick three-piece suits and Porsches. And who would have believed that this lovely country bloke would be so damned good in bed? An involuntary smile crept up on her. Her weekend demon lover.

A fantasy come true.

It was taken for granted they would see each other again that evening. Fraser appeared in time for dinner showered and freshly shaved and she caught that long-ago scent of Old Spice as he followed her into the kitchen. There, he handed over a rectangular wrapped package.

'Thought you might like this, Maddy.'

She could feel him watching her expectantly as she folded back the wrapping. Somehow she managed to keep her expression neutral. 'Oh, Fraser . . . you – you shouldn't have.'

And, as she took in the dreadfully executed oil of some banal country scene, she meant it. God, it was truly awful.

'Got it at a craft shop. Thought it might re-mind you of around here while you're in the city.'

He expected her to take it back to *Sydney* with her? Maddy had to stifle a horrified giggle.

'Oh, I think it'd suit this place better, Fraser.' She glanced vaguely around. 'Guess I'll have to think where to put it.' Like hell she would.

They ate on the verandah, sharing a bottle of wine.

'I'm glad you're here, Fraser, because this is a very special occasion,' He looked up at her, feeling an unexpected tightening in his belly.

Then, with an arch smile she dug her fork into the bowl of salad and held aloft a slice of tomato. 'My first crop of tomatoes!'

Playing along, he raised his glass in amused acknowledgement. 'Here's to primary producer of the year.'

When they'd finished eating they sat in easy silence in the warm night air. Maddy enjoyed the fact that neither of them felt the need to talk. What had happened between them had happened. They had no need to analyse it. The same way they felt no compulsion to make small talk for no reason.

From where he sat close beside her, Fraser began to trail long, cool fingers down her arm. It wasn't long before desire licked inside her and caught alight, and without a word Maddy stood up, put out her hand, and led him into the bedroom.

'You're beautiful, Maddy.' He whispered the words in her ear as he unbuttoned her blouse, unhooked her bra.

The quiet confidence of his actions excited her. Still fully dressed, he was sitting on the edge of the bed, his eyes glazed with longing, and she shivered as his hands caressed the swell of her hips, the curve of her buttocks, the still firm globes of her breasts. It was the tantalizing slowness of the seduction that heated her blood.

And Fraser O'Neill knew it.

Everything seemed different now when she wasn't there. He went about his work as before but Maddy dominated his thoughts to the exclusion of all else. He imagined himself touching her warm flesh, stroking the small depression at the base of her throat, breathing in the scent of her tangled hair. His mind played out a thousand imaginary conversations. And he found himself dreaming crazy dreams . . .

The gallery was always busy in the run-up to Christmas and for that Maddy was grateful. She hated Christmas. She wished she could be brave or foolish enough to take a pill that would knock her out for the entire three or four days when everyone else in the world seemed to be revelling in love and family. It was a myth she knew, but that didn't help her feel any better about being alone.

Her mother was still alive but her deterioration in the last couple of years had been painful for Maddy to watch. Alzheimers was no respecter of class or intellect or achievement and Maddy was a tormented spectator as her mother curled away to a mindless stranger who existed in some terrible dimension without a past, a present or a future.

But even though it had been a long while now since Irene Reynolds had recognised her daughter, Maddy would make her usual visit to the nursing home before leaving town for the Christmas break. They had been close and her mother was all she had.

It was every bit as terrible as she remembered. The vacant eyes, the silent withdrawal, the rare and heartbreaking moments of animation when her mother would start a garbled relating of some incident from three decades ago as if it had happened yesterday.

When she could bear it no longer Maddy got to her feet. 'I'm going now, Mum.' Her lips brushed softly against the white, baby soft hair.

Jerking away from her touch, Irene Reynolds glared up angrily from her hospital chair. 'Don't touch me! Get away from me!'

Afterwards, partly to snap herself out of the depression that inevitably followed such visits, and partly because they hadn't seen each other for a while, Maddy had arranged to meet Meg and Jane for a Christmas drink.

'Is she worse?' Jane asked sympathetically, as the three of them sat with a bottle of Moet in the atrium bar of an inner city hotel.

Maddy shrugged. 'What's *worse*?'

It was clear to Jane that she should change the subject. 'You're not really spending Christmas alone up there are you Maddy? You've got heaps of friends here who'd –'

'I'm looking forward to it.' Maddy had grown a little tired of those single friend boozy Christmas lunches in expensive hotels.

'I'll swap with you,' Jane said heavily. 'You can go to my mother. Just say the word. I spend the money for an airline ticket home and all she does is put me down from the moment I walk in the door. Target practice, that's all I've ever been. Jane, why do you wear your skirts so short? Why do you do your hair like that? Jane, no man's going to fall for a woman who drinks so much. Blah, blah, blah.'

'Is Lauren going to be there?' Meg asked as she topped up their glasses.

'Are you kidding? Far too sensible. She's staying in London. Better the freezing cold and a Whimpy Bar than Christmas with Grandmama – not that we're allowed to call her that, mind you.'

Maddy sipped at her drink and wondered how different her Christmas might be if she'd been the mother of a twenty-year-old daughter. And she allowed herself to think of all those other Christmases when she too might have been chasing around the stores buying Barbies and jewellery sets and clothes and records. And of the other things that missing out on motherhood had cost her like ballet and piano lessons, exams and first dates.

But it wasn't good to dwell on all that. Not when it brought to mind that September morning when she and Alex had found their way to the very private entrance of that anonymous terrace house. They had got the address the way people usually did back then. Word of mouth. From other unmarried students faced, like themselves, with the same terrifying problem.

While Alex waited they'd taken her away to do what needed to be done. She'd had only the vaguest idea what might happen and was trembling with fear. Then: stirruped feet, the drag and scrape of callous metal, the blood, the pain and nausea.

And afterwards, the envelope slipped into a white pocket, and back to Alex's room in the shared student household. There, shivering and sobbing, Maddy had clung to him while he held and stroked her and quietly did his best to talk away her guilt.

'We did the right thing, Maddy. We're only eighteen. I promise you, sweetheart, there'll be time later for other babies.'

But there hadn't been. Alex's illness had made sure of that. And so Maddy tried not to think about how she had rid herself of the only bit of Alex that might still have lived on for her. Tried not to think of the 23-year-old daughter with whom she might have laughed and exchanged presents on Christmas morning.

Many years later when contraception failed and it happened again, Maddy had done the same thing. This time with cold pragmatism, no guilt. She reasoned that if she had missed out on having Alex's child, there was no way she would bear the child of a man whose name she barely knew when she slipped into his bed. Not looking for love, not hoping for passion. Merely reminding herself how it felt to be touched and held by another human being.

'I'm going on a cruise. Six days by myself.' Meg interrupted the drift of her thoughts. 'The boys are going to their father. I hate every second Christmas.'

And Maddy realised there were other ways of suffering. All those women she knew who had gone into marriage full of hope and trust and joy. Who, after so many years, had got used to a houseful of family. When it ended how did they adapt to the sudden shattering silence of an empty house? When women were born, she wondered, did they get stamped with the visa to their particular mode of suffering?

Then she thought of Fraser. And knew that men weren't immune either.

Later, as the three friends kissed goodbye, wishing each other a 'merry Christmas', Jane paused and studied her warmly. 'You're looking well, Maddy. Country life must agree with you. How're you getting on with the sexy neighbour? If it's open season let me know, won't you?'

Maddy smiled and shook her head. 'Get serious, Jane.'

What was going on with Fraser was nobody's business but her own.

She did her best to leave in time to beat the worst of the Christmas exodus. The hamper she'd picked up from David Jones should sustain her, she figured, if the shops were closed over the break.

She knew that Fraser had some Rotary do on that evening and his Christmas plans were to spend three or four days with his daughter's family on the coast. But they were seeing each other tomorrow before he left. 'I'm taking you on a picnic, Maddy,' he'd said when they'd parted the week before. 'Somewhere special.'

'Sounds good. But let me pack the lunch.'

Despite her earlier departure the traffic was heavier than usual with Christmas-laden cars and swaying campervans. There was also the familiar holiday atmosphere of gathering excitement which Maddy found depressing.

Yet as soon as she opened the cottage door and stepped inside the house her mood lightened. She felt cocooned. Safe from the world outside with its tacit message that single people did not really belong – at least not at this time of the year.

Back again in her simple, comfortable haven Maddy felt almost light-headed with relief. Let the world have their damn Christmas she thought. She'd manage just fine.

She was ready when he arrived at mid-morning. Now, when she looked at Fraser she imagined the fit, hard body under his jeans and shirt, the feel of his hands as they touched her the way she loved to be touched, the taste and scent of him, the erotic magic that left her breathless and sated.

'How are you, Maddy?' He looked up at the verandah. She was smiling, her fair hair shining in the sunshine and he revelled in the jolt of pleasure that shot through him whenever he saw her anew. The straight-backed confidence, the fine, pale skin, the intelligent blue-grey eyes that hinted at more than she realised. Maybe one day, he thought, she would tell him about the shadows that lay beneath their surface beauty.

Without replying Maddy walked up to him, slid her arms around his neck and opened her mouth to his.

Fraser's heart bounced off his ribs and only when they finally drew apart did it feel as if he'd started breathing again.

'This lunch?' His voice was unsteady as he pointed to the Esky. Distracting himself.

'How's your appetite?' She was teasing him.

'Insatiable.' With a grin he picked up the heavy cooler and carried it to the truck.

The creek ran under a fringe of lacy willows, then widened into a green pool beside a sandy bank.

'I can't imagine being anywhere else,' said Maddy, her face dappled by the canopy of leaves. They had eaten their chicken and salad lunch and were lying back on the rug-covered tarpaulin.

'Yeah, you don't need much more than this in life do you?'

Propped up on one elbow Fraser watched a dragonfly skim the surface of the water. 'Used to swim here as a boy. Mum always knew where to find me on a hot day.'

They had bumped their way over rough tracks and paddocks to arrive at this spot which had once been part of the original O'Neill property. It was a place of tranquil beauty, the soothing murmur of the creek mingling with the gentle hum of insects and the rustle of a hot breeze through the eucalypts. Maddy could imagine children catching tadpoles, swinging off willow branches, floating on the surface of that cool, dark water.

She felt she knew Fraser well enough now to give voice to her recurrent thought. 'It must have been terrible to lose all this. I mean, you must wish your grandchildren could be playing here now, don't you?'

For a long moment he said nothing and she wondered if she should apologise for having touched too raw a nerve, when – 'If I've learned anything Maddy, it's not to waste time with regrets. Life's about looking forward, not getting stuck in what might have been.'

She felt an unexpected spasm of irritation. The simple man's philosophy. Except that simple, homespun words couldn't tell her how to forget that Alex had ever existed. Or how to let go of the pain.

In place of a reply she closed her eyes and felt the warmth of the sun on her lids.

Maybe he had sensed her mood, for the next moment Maddy felt the touch of his hand on her neck. Her eyes flickered open and met those of the man beside her.

Fraser O'Neill said gently. 'Life doesn't have to be complicated, Maddy.'

From the start Fraser had sensed a complexity to Maddy Tyler that he still did not understand. He had no intention of rushing her but his words hung in the air, inviting confidence.

With a barely discernible shake of her head Maddy looked away. It had never been made easier by talking.

Beside her, Fraser sensed her sadness. It enveloped her in an almost palpable shroud. As he waited for some sort of response, a ray of sunshine suddenly found its way through the branches and showed him the fine lines around her mouth and eyes. Lines etched not only by time but also by pain . . .

The silence held. He hesitated, then lowered his lips to hers, less in a gesture of passion than of comfort and sympathy. For what, Fraser wasn't exactly sure. The kiss lasted, grew warmer, and slowly he felt her tension begin to slip away. Gently he moved his body over hers, shuddering as he felt her slim arms slide around his neck and draw him close.

Beneath him, Maddy relished the weight of her lover's body. I need this, she told herself. I need sex and comfort and gentleness. I need what this warm, uncomplicated man can give me.

'I hate leaving you to Christmas alone.' They were back at the cottage saying goodbye. Fraser was heading off early the next morning. 'If there was any way of staying I would. But my daughter's expecting me.'

Maddy shot him a look of surprise. She would never have expected him to change his plans, had no desire to disrupt the tenor of his normal life.

'It's just another day, Fraser. I'll be fine.' Smiling, she squeezed his hand and said lightly, 'And thanks for the wonderful Christmas present.' She was referring to their afternoon. To the hungry and uninhibited lovemaking that had left them both brimming with sensual pleasure.

'You're wonderful.' He bent forward and gave her a final gentle kiss, breathed in her perfume, tasted her skin, stored the sensations for the days they would be apart. 'See you soon.'

Three days.

As he drove away Fraser felt as if he had stepped inside a new reality. A kaleidoscope of sensation where he breathed more deeply, saw more clearly, felt more truly.

He had never imagined it could happen again. But Maddy Tyler had come into his life and she was everything he needed and wanted.

CHAPTER ELEVEN

The sound sawed through the thick forest of her sleep. Maddy blinked awake. The noise came again. Someone sounding a car horn. And close.

With a sleepy murmur she rolled over and checked the time on the bedside alarm. God. Barely six. What idiot needed to wake people up at this obscene hour? And, she suddenly remembered, on Christmas Day of all days?

The insistent sound came again and Maddy realised it was coming from the front of the house. Irritated, she dragged herself out of bed, padded over to the window and pulled back the drapes. Below, on the front drive, she saw Fraser's pick-up, the engine still running.

By the open driver's door, Fraser stood looking up at the house. He caught sight of her and waved. With a frown, Maddy pushed open the window but Fraser called out before she could speak.

'Sorry to wake you! I'm on my way to Joy's but had to stop and drop in your Christmas present. At the front door. Better not leave it too long in the sun!' With a smile and wave he climbed into the pick-up and left her watching him drive off.

A present. Hell. Maddy had deliberated about that but in the end had decided to avoid the implications of getting something for Fraser.

As she walked through the house barefooted, dressed only in her knee-length cotton nightie, she guessed she should have made the gesture – since Fraser obviously had. But, she yawned, if he'd had to, why couldn't he have given it to her yesterday, at a civilised hour?

As she turned the key in the deadlock, a strange sound reached her ears. Then she opened the door and caught her breath in surprise.

There, tied to the verandah post was a little creature with floppy ears and a long pink tongue lolling out from a row of sharp baby teeth.

'Oh, *no* . . .' Maddy spoke the words aloud as the pup yelped in delight at her appearance, leaping and straining at its lead. One of Girlie's pups. It had to be. The others had all been given away so this must be the one Fraser had been going to keep for himself.

Maddy felt a warm rush of exasperation. How in the world did he expect her to look after a pup? She couldn't take it back to Sydney with her. And anyway, she didn't *want* a dog. Didn't need this sort of responsibility in her life. Why the hell hadn't Fraser checked with her first!

Angry and irritated, she moved to untie the animal's lead from the post when she saw an envelope tucked under the rug that lay folded beside a battered cooler.

Ignoring the puppy's squeals Maddy slit the envelope open and read the Christmas card it contained. Along with his best wishes Fraser had added, 'Now I won't have to think of you spending Christmas Day alone. Girlie and I can look after her during the week so don't worry about that. She's twelve weeks old and housetrained so I've made it easy for you! I called her Kelly but that's up to you. PS Plenty of meat in the cooler.'

'I don't believe this,' Maddy muttered aloud as she looked down at the energetic bundle of fur at her feet. 'I just don't believe it.'

And she resolved that the moment Fraser returned he would be resuming delivery of his ill-considered gift.

'Want another, Dad?'

Fraser had arrived around midday and was now sitting with his daughter in the shady backyard of her coastal home. Nearby, his two grandsons were splashing in their wading pool watched by a panting Girlie.

'No thanks, love, that was just fine.' Fraser bent to put his empty cup on the lawn by his feet.

'Here, I'll take it.' Joy stood up, held out her hand. She stacked his cup and saucer with her own on the wooden tray alongside the remains of an iced chocolate cake that was starting to melt in the heat. 'I'd better take all this inside. Keep an eye on the kids for a sec.'

As his daughter carried the tray back into the house, Fraser followed her with his eyes. Joy had got his height, but her dark hair and pretty eyes were definitely her mother's. She was twenty-six this year, he calculated. Hard to believe. The lucky one. The baby who had gone the distance. And brought them such delight. Even as a teenager, Joy had given them no trouble and she'd always been close to her mother. He remembered how Nancy had spent the first month with her when their first grandchild had been born. It had been the only time they'd been separated through all the years of their marriage.

His practice run at the loneliness to come, Fraser thought. But no preparation for a loss that was permanent and final.

Joy had just fallen pregnant with their second grandchild when Nancy died. He remembered how, the night before the funeral, Joy had sobbed wildly against his chest. 'She'll never get to see this one, Dad! She'll never hold my baby in her arms!'

He pushed the unhappy thought away as his daughter rejoined him. He could tell just by looking that she was content. Mike was a good father, a caring husband. Liked a few too many occasionally, but Fraser was sure Joy knew how to handle that. She wasn't one to put up with things if they didn't suit. She spoke her mind and Mike fell into line.

'So what's new, Dad?' Joy pulled her chair back into the retreating shade and resettled herself beside him.

'Not much, love. Same old thing.'

'You're looking well so things must be going okay.' Joy couldn't remember the last time her father had appeared so animated and happy. It was good to see.

It was all Fraser could do not to tell her about Maddy. From the moment he'd arrived he'd been longing to speak about the miracle that had taken place in his life. But he knew the time wasn't right. It was too soon to tell Joy. He'd have to prepare her for the revelation that he had found someone with whom he wanted to share his life.

'Did that hail storm do much damage in the end?' The newspapers had reported the sudden destructive storm and the effect it might have on the grape crop.

Damage . . . Oh, no, he wouldn't call it damage.

Aloud he said, 'Not in my neck of the woods, thank goodness. And it brought some good rain at last. Though a bit too late in the growing season. It's my bet volume'll be down but quality up.'

'I wish you'd give it all away and move out here near us, Dad. You're tied to that place. We don't see enough of you.'

'You know how it is, love. But I promise, this next year I'll definitely make the time to get up more often.'

He nodded at his grandsons. 'Might find myself learning to ride a surf board with those two yet.'

Those placatory words suddenly suffused him with guilt. Because Fraser couldn't imagine spending his weekends away from Maddy.

After Christmas lunch he offered to take the boys to the beach, and Joy and Mike were grateful for the break. 'Just keep putting the blockout on them, Dad,' his daughter cautioned as they packed into the family station wagon.

At four, on their way back to the house, the two little boys were too tired to notice when he pulled over at a public telephone box.

Heart starting to thump, Fraser stood in the hot, glass cabinet and listened to the ringing tone at the other end. When he finally heard her voice his spirits leapt.

'Maddy, it's me, Fraser. Just wanted to wish you Merry Christmas on the right day. What did you think of your present?'

God, he was garbling on like a teenage kid.

'Fraser,' she didn't even try to hide her exasperation, 'look, I know you meant well, but I can't have a dog. It's impossible. I'm only here part of –'

'I know all that. I'll look after her in between times. I just thought the company'd be good for you.'

'Fraser,' her voice was cool. 'I've managed by myself for a pretty damn long time now. I don't want the *responsibility* of a dog. I don't want anything that's dependent on me. That's not the way I live my life. So, while I appreciate the thought I just can't take on a dog, okay?'

There was a long silence and she thought for a moment he'd hung up.

In the steamy cubicle Fraser felt the sweat beading his face. 'Maddy, I'm sorry. I didn't mean to upset you. Of course if it's a problem I'll take her back the minute I'm home. Don't worry about it.' The sweat was trickling into his eyes. 'I'll see you soon. Merry Christmas, Maddy.'

He hung up, and at the other end of the line Maddy Tyler stood blinking back tears, feeling like the worst, most confused, icy-hearted bitch.

There was the usual garbage on television Christmas night and Maddy turned off the set in disgust. On the coffee table beside her stood a glass and an almost empty bottle of expensive white wine. Ah, yes, the years had taught her how to handle Christmas. The perfect way to fast forward the loneliest day of the year.

She looked at her watch. Eight-thirty. Too early for bed. The pup, curled up on its blanket in the corner, rested its fluffy head on its paws, and watched her.

'Come on.' Maddy rose to her feet. 'I'd better let you out a minute.' Responding to her voice, the little animal was immediately alert. Ears pricked and tail high, it followed her to the door.

The night sky looked like the soft, dark jewellery pad in some expensive store scattered with diamonds of varying sizes and light. 'Go on!' Maddy shooed the pup towards the steps. It hesitated, looking up at her and she waved her hands at it again. 'I said, go on!'

This time the dog made her clumsy way down into the yard while Maddy stretched out on the top step and waited.

So. She'd survived another Christmas Day. This time without her usual buffer of other determinedly happy fellow singles. Just a dog.

She gave a drunken giggle. Should she consider that a step forwards, or backwards? Animals in place of humans . . . And, without warning, a sob bubbled through her fragile mirth. Her eyes swam with tears. She'd tried so hard! Why couldn't she forget how those Christmases had felt when she'd had someone to love, to share with, to give her sanctuary and warmth. A reason for living.

Grief swelling inside her like some poisonous miasma, Maddy buried her face in trembling fingers. 'Oh, Alex . . . Alex . . .' Rocking back and forth like a helpless child she tore herself apart thinking of what might have been, the years she had been cheated of.

Until something wet and cold pressed against her cheek and made her raise her tear-stained face. She had forgotten the pup. The little animal whimpered and looked at her with quizzical dark eyes. Maddy drew the small, furry body into her arms and clung weeping to her only companion on that dying Christmas night.

It was after dusk on Boxing Day evening when Fraser turned into the drive that led to the cottage.

Recognising the sound of the pick-up, Maddy appeared looking puzzled at the cottage door.

'Fraser! I thought you weren't going to be back until tomorrow.'

That's what Joy had thought too and it had caused a moment of awkwardness at their parting when he'd had to make up some guilty excuse about the traffic. But all he could think of was seeing Maddy again.

Now he leapt up the steps and folded her in a bear hug. 'I missed you.' Simple words. Not those that were bursting in his throat – *You were all I thought about every waking hour.*

For somehow Fraser knew that Maddy Tyler was still not ready to hear anything like that. He sensed the brittleness in her still, the barriers that still had to be dismantled. But it would happen, he told himself. He just had to be patient.

She looked up into that warm honest smile, the blue eyes that were even more striking in his tanned, rugged face. 'I was just going to have a sandwich but now I'll cook something. Have you eaten?'

While she prepared a meal he apologised for the surprise that had gone wrong. 'I'm sorry about the pup, Maddy. I guess I should have checked with you first.'

'Well . . . I'm sorry too, Fraser.' She tried to make up for her bluntness on the telephone. 'It was sweet of you, but I hope you understand.'

And then the same simple routine. Dinner on the verandah. A bottle of wine. The two dogs at their feet.

Her laugh carried on the hot, still air as he told her about his grandsons, the size of their eyes when he kept pulling coin after coin from his Christmas pudding. 'Told them I must've got the right serving. After that they spent the rest of the afternoon sifting the rest of the pudding to bits!'

While she cleared the plates he poured the last of the wine and they finished it in companionable silence.

Fraser shifted in his seat, felt the shirt sticking to his back. 'It's a hot one tonight.' It was after ten but the temperature had barely dropped. 'Heard on the car radio they had a big fire on the South Coast. Guess it's that time of year.'

Taking her cue, Maddy stood up. Reaching out a hand she said quietly, 'And now it's this time of the night.'

She'd planned to stay at the cottage until just after New Year. During those days she fell in easily enough with Fraser's suggestions of visits to vineyards and craft shops, of yabby fishing and picnics.

One evening she even allowed him to take her to dinner in some out-of-the-way restaurant. A place where she could be sure no one she knew would be likely to see them. While she'd take a bet there was gossip among the locals, that didn't mean it had to reach Sydney.

On New Year's Eve Maddy prepared a cold meal and they ate outside as usual as they waited for one year to end and another to begin.

It was the night that Maddy always hated couples. With their stroke-of-midnight kisses promising each other another twelve months of comfort, support, sharing. Her lips hardened into a tight scimitar of cynicism. Ah, yes, the one moment of the year that she allowed herself the indulgence of romantic illusion. For couldn't she make a list of the couples she knew who had split in the last twelve months? While she remained safe in her cell of singledom. No one to leave her, betray her, undermine her, die on her . . .

'I can hear your brain buzzing from here. Going to share it with me?'

Turning, she smiled at the warm, uncomplicated man beside her. Somehow she figured that Fraser O'Neill didn't deserve to share her cynicism.

She gave a brief shake of her head and a moment later pushed herself out of her chair. 'Just a sec.'

Glass in hand, Fraser watched as she entered the living room through the open french doors. He loved the way her body moved when she walked. The easy grace and unconscious sensuality. And he blessed again his good fortune in sharing with her this most nostalgic of nights. The start of another year. A new beginning for them both . . .

The next moment a slow, sweet ballad began to play softly and evocatively through the stereo speakers. His breath caught when she reappeared naked and beautiful, holding out her hand. Without a word he stood and took her in his arms, pressing his hand into the curve of her back and drawing her close. Feeling like he had found the reason for being alive.

They made little pretence of dancing, barely moving to the soft murmur of the music while the molten flow of desire crept through their limbs.

And when the music came to an end they moved down the darkened hallway to the bedroom. In the soft glow of the bedside lamp Maddy unbuttoned his shirt, pushed him down on the bed and Fraser caught the scent of perfume and desire as she pulled off his jeans. Then he was sliding over her nakedness, feeling the soft pillows of her breasts, drugging himself with the salty warmth of her skin.

Only much later did they realise that midnight had come and gone.

And it was not long after that that Fraser asked softly, recklessly, 'Will you tell me, Maddy, what it was that hurt you so much?'

CHAPTER TWELVE

It happened in two short hours. Soaring temperatures, dry blustery winds, and an igniting spark – perhaps from wind-whipped powerlines.

Fraser was called out along with all other members of the Rural Fire Brigade. The sheet of flames advanced quickly and by mid afternoon thirty volunteers and professionals were fighting the leaping, roaring blaze on three different fronts.

For the first time Maddy truly realised how rapidly the beauty of the bush could be transformed into a life-threatening zone of blistering heat, acrid smoke, swirling ash and cinders. That realisation was reinforced even further when, late in the day, with the fires showing no signs of abating, it was clear that her own and other nearby properties were at risk.

All the tired fire fighters could do was hope that by evening the winds would drop sufficiently to enable them to carry out a controlled backburn to starve the main blaze of further fuel.

As the fire front moved closer Maddy volunteered her own home as a control centre. By six that evening her kitchen was full of an ever-changing parade of grubby-faced men in brightly coloured overalls and teams of stoic local women who had arrived with supplies of food and cold drinks and were now helping to make endless plates of sandwiches.

An hour after dark Fraser, barely recognisable under a mask of ash and grime, arrived in the crowded kitchen with the news that the back-burn had begun. 'The wind hasn't really dropped enough,' he reported between gulps of cold water, 'but that's a risk we've got to take.'

As he spoke he looked across the room to where Maddy stood side by side with the other women busily buttering rounds of bread. She looked tired but he saw no sign of fear on her face. As if, Fraser thought, she had been born and bred in the country, had grown used to handling this sort of emergency. Maddy Tyler was an amazing woman in more ways than one.

'Have a sandwich, Fraser.' It was Del, smiling as she proffered him an overflowing plate.

'Thanks, Del.' Grabbing a handful he ate quickly before refilling his water flask at the sink. Then, manoeuvring across the crowded kitchen, he reached Maddy's side.

'You okay?' Without conscious thought he placed a grimy hand on her shoulder. Remembering that this was a woman who, just a few short months ago, had been seriously ill.

Looking up at him, Maddy nodded and smiled. 'Fine, Fraser. Just take care out there, okay?'

Curious eyes besides Del's recorded the intimate exchange.

Two days after the emergency was over Maddy returned to Sydney. As she drove down the freeway towards the Harbour Bridge and sunlit water a smile twitched around her lips.

Hell, Christmas holidays in the bush. Why, she wondered? Why the heat and dust, the fire and the stress instead of some five star resort with pristine swimming pools, airconditioned rooms and Margaritas?

Her grin grew wider. It was the best damn Christmas holiday she'd had in years.

Over the next six weeks Maddy acknowledged the existence of an important new balance in her life. The yin and the yang. A sense of peace.

She still worked harder than most but her attitude had altered. When she came up against the inevitable problems and stresses that went with running a business she found herself handling them with a new sense of patience and serenity. Calm acceptance had replaced impatience.

The joy of regular sex, she joked to herself as she pondered her change of outlook. And the restful surroundings of her weekend hideaway.

In February, when she saw her specialist for her check up, she was given a clean bill of health.

'You've made an excellent recovery, Maddy. Keep that stress factor under control and I don't think you'll have too many problems in the future.'

It was exactly what she planned to do.

The tenor of her life fell into a pattern that suited her well. The city, work and Tony. The cottage and Fraser. The balance she had been searching for.

Jane made her own guess to the reasons behind the new glow on her friend's face. And with her usual bluntness said, 'Darling, you're getting it, aren't you? Don't lie to me, I can always tell. It's the cowboy, isn't it?' With a delighted laugh she put an arm around Maddy's waist.

Both had felt obliged to attend the opening night party for the latest effort by an old friend, now one of the country's leading playwrights. Some sort of African music beat steadily in the background and the acrid smoke of cigarettes and dope sliced into Maddy's country-clean nostrils.

'With that imagination, Jane, you're wasted as an editor.' Maddy smiled.

But for once Jane made no joke in return. There was concern in her voice as she said, 'Seriously, Maddy, I can see the cottage has done you good, but I hope you're not going to lose touch with the rest of us. We do love you, you know.'

Surprised and touched, Maddy replied with a quick reassuring hug. 'You've been a wonderful friend to me, Jane. Nothing will ever change that.' And she meant it.

Later as she was thinking of leaving she felt a tap on her shoulder. 'How've you been Maddy? Missed seeing you around.'

Refiring her social boilers she turned to greet a craggy faced man whose olive skin and shaved head gave him a passing resemblance to Yul Brynner. Tim Chester had made his fortune from the international demand for Aboriginal native art.

'I'm out of town a bit these days, Tim.'

'Yeah, I heard. You back on top of things now? Must be, you're looking great.'

'Thanks. I feel it.'

Tim Chester lowered his voice. 'I guess you heard about Neville Tobin?'

'Neville?' Maddy felt a stab of guilt. She'd been out of touch with friends like Neville and Luke for too long. Especially given the circumstances.

Tim Chester raised an eyebrow. 'He's really on the downhill slide now.'

'Oh, God . . .' Maddy silently berated herself. 'I'll give him a call,' she promised.

Fraser hated Sydney. If he was lucky he only had to come to the place once or twice a year. He understood how some people could enjoy the noise and bustle, the entertainment and shopping, but he wouldn't dream of changing his lifestyle for any of it.

Today's trip was unexpected. A last minute favour to pick up Sam Kruger's son who was arriving on the afternoon train from Melbourne.

Sam's own truck had broken down that morning and he'd had to take it into Cessnock for repairs.

But much as he'd been glad enough to help a friend, Fraser admitted to himself that another part of it had been the unexpected opportunity to see Maddy. On her home ground. And he had timed his journey in the hope that she might let him take her to lunch. A surprise, he thought.

Only as he was heading over the Bridge did he start to have second thoughts. Maddy led a busy life, he knew. If he'd done the right thing he should have called her instead of just dropping in.

With the help of an out-of-date street directory Fraser finally found his way through the maze of streets to the narrow lane where he managed to spot the black and white sign announcing the location of the Tyler Gallery. After that, it meant a slow crawl around the block until someone was kind enough to leave him a parking spot. In a small nearby milk bar he found a pay phone that worked and rang her business number. But the line was continually engaged.

Fraser looked at his watch. If he cut it too fine he wouldn't make it back to the railway station on time. So. He'd take a chance. Call in unannounced.

As he made his way up the slight incline of the street he checked his reflection in a shop window. Even though it was hot he'd worn a jacket.

Maddy heard the door swing open as she stood talking to one of her customers. Tony, she knew, was busy on the telephone in the back office.

Then, from the corner of her eye she realised there was something very familiar about that tall, lean figure and the thick, salt-and-pepper hair.

Maddy lost the thread of what she was saying. Her well-heeled customer, noting her reaction, turned and followed the direction of her gaze. Fraser smiled at both women, lifted his hand in a friendly greeting, at the same time indicating he was happy to wait.

Maddy, distracted, wound up her conversation as smoothly and quickly as possible. As soon as she had ushered her customer out of the front door she turned her frowning attention to Fraser.

'Fraser, what's wrong? Has something happened?'

He started to explain, at the same time taking in the slim-fitting red suit, the fancy gold necklace, the high heeled shoes. He'd never seen her dressed like this. She looked . . . well, like a model in one of those glossy magazines . . . inaccessible, untouchable. And her polite, distant expression only added to the impression.

'I'm sorry I didn't give you any warning,' he repeated. 'But do you think you might have time to have a bite with me?'

She took a deep breath, nervously hoping Tony wouldn't suddenly appear from the back office. 'Look, give me a minute, there's a couple of things I still have to do. There's a coffee shop on the next corner, why don't you wait there and I'll be out as soon as I can get away.'

The pleasure was obvious in his smile and blue eyes. 'Sure. That's okay. I'm just glad that you've got a little time to spare.'

Maddy waited, watching until he had walked past the gallery window and out of sight, and hating herself for her shallowness. What sort of snob had she become that Fraser's unexpected appearance on her home territory should throw her so off balance? What made things so different here?

She went off to make some excuse to Tony.

Later that evening she had more time to think about her disturbing reaction to Fraser's unannounced appearance.

They'd eaten in a small nondescript Italian restaurant where she had never been before and was unlikely to bump into anyone she knew.

It was hard to admit, but Fraser's intrusion into her normal everyday life had made her very uncomfortable.

Come *on*, Maddy, she berated herself. Just where are you coming from? The guy's okay to sleep with but not to be seen out with?

The realisation upset her, forcing her to once again confront the ugliness of her own shallow snobbery. It was true. Fraser O'Neill was an attractive man. He had surprised and thrilled her in bed. And she enjoyed his company.

But as part of that other world. Not the one she was entrenched in here.

This was a man, she told herself, who had spent all his life in a country town. He couldn't tell a poster from a print, had probably never heard of Chomsky or Mamet or Magritte.

Which was no problem when all she was after was a simple, uncomplicated weekend affair.

But no basis for anything else.

It was in that split second that Maddy realised for the first time what she should have seen long before.

She'd just assumed that Fraser was looking at this thing between them as she did. Great sex, someone to laugh with, share a meal with. Not for a moment had she dreamed that he'd read more into it than that.

And now, she saw, he had.

Irritated and guilty at the same time, Maddy knew she would have to do something. Make him understand that she had always meant to keep this casual, that she had her life and he had his, and there couldn't be any expectations or demands.

And the best way to do that was to curtail her regular visits to the cottage.

CHAPTER THIRTEEN

It was Stewart Conachie driving home from a night's roo shooting who saw Fraser's pick-up leaving the old cottage in the early hours.

Word didn't take long to reach Del. Not with all the help it received along the way. But Del hadn't needed it to confirm her suspicions. Even if she hadn't seen the way Fraser had touched Maddy Tyler the night of the fire she'd still have known that something serious was going on.

It had been weeks since Fraser had put in an appearance at the club on Friday nights, and most weekends no one saw hide nor hair of him in town.

She'd enquired of course, rung him a few times, but Fraser's excuses – 'too busy', 'too tired' – had been hardly convincing.

No, she thought, Fraser O'Neill had never been a liar and he was too old to start now.

Del found herself cursing her patience, her reluctance to rush things. Now she'd been beaten to the punch by a woman who could never appreciate the man Fraser was, who'd never treat him with the respect and caring he deserved.

She did her best to convince herself that the affair would blow over. Fraser just wasn't the type to fit into the life of someone like Maddy Tyler. The woman was playing with him. Using him. She probably slept with whoever came along and it didn't mean a thing.

As she pondered that particular line of reasoning Del found herself flooded with a purity of purpose. Fraser had to be saved from himself. From the hurt and humiliation that was sure to follow. He was out of his depth with a woman like Maddy Tyler.

Now all Del had to do was figure out the best means of carrying out the rescue.

'I wasn't sure if I should tell you or not, love, but maybe things are getting more out of hand than you know. That sort of woman'll just use him and discard him when it suits her.'

'But – Dad wouldn't be interested in someone like that, Del. Surely.' Over the line Del could hear the incredulity in Joy's voice.

'It's not so much your Dad, love. Seems to me it's her who's making all the moves.' Del let that one sink in. 'Any chance you can come down for a day or so? Then you'd see things for yourself.'

'It's not that easy with the kids . . .'

'I hate to see your Dad made a fool of, Joy.'

The newspaper clippings from Del arrived a few days later. One was a feature on high-profile successful businesswomen, another pictured Maddy Tyler with her latest artistic 'find' and a couple had been taken at various social events with Maddy in the company of well-dressed, wealthy looking businessmen.

As Joy studied the grainy photograph of the elegant blonde, her face creased in a frown.

Her father was in his early fifties. It was only natural that sooner or later he might think of marrying again. And she had no objection to that. Of course no one would ever be able to replace her mother but that didn't mean she wanted Fraser to be alone for the rest of his life.

If anything, Joy had half hoped that Del Bradley might be the one to finally tempt him out of his solitary existence. They'd been friends, all of them, when her mother was alive, and Del was the same age and well liked in the town. It would be good for her father to have someone to look after him again, to be with a woman who understood him and who'd be there for him as he got older.

But of one thing Joy was certain. This career type from Sydney wasn't the one to offer him any of that.

Her face tightened as she folded the clippings and put them back into the envelope. She could see very clearly now what Del had been getting at. Her father was still a good looking man, and a woman like Maddy Tyler – who had everything else – could be after only one thing.

Well, Joy determined, whatever it took she wasn't going to see her father hurt.

It was Wednesday evening when Maddy made the call. She'd never phoned him from the city before.

'. . . just to ask if you'd keep an eye on the place, Fraser. Looks like I'm going to be stuck here for the next couple of weekends. Work's just frantic.' She spoke quickly, eager to make her point and leave it at that. 'Kelly okay?'

'Just fine, Maddy. Asleep at my feet . . .' His voice softened. 'Don't push yourself too hard, will you?' A pause. 'I'll miss you.'

'Bye, Fraser.'

The short conversation over, Fraser felt disappointment settle in him like a lead weight. When the young dog awoke and sidled up for attention he stroked her soft fur without any real awareness of his actions.

Maddy's call had made him realise just how much he'd come to rely on and look forward to their weekends together. In just a few months they'd moved from friends to lovers, and Maddy had become a very important part of his life.

And Fraser had dared to hope she might become an equally important part of his future. Not that he kidded himself it would be all plain sailing. That day in the city when he'd taken her to lunch he'd clearly sensed her unease. For the first time he had been on her territory and she hadn't quite known how to handle it. If he was honest, Fraser knew snobbery had something to do with it. But for all that, he had seen enough to know that there was a deeper woman inside. If Maddy could only drop her guard, stop worrying about things that didn't matter, she might find life a whole lot less complicated than she sometimes made it.

Over the next two weekends Maddy felt both disappointed and resentful about being deprived of the haven she'd grown used to and the man whose company and body she had grown to enjoy. As she hung around her apartment she found she had also grown accustomed to the quiet companionship of Kelly. And admitting to that dependency only upset her further.

But as long as it cooled things off, she told herself. Made Fraser see she was determined to keep everything casual. He'd have time to get things in perspective and, she hoped, pick up the threads of his regular social life.

And if he didn't take the hint? Maddy could hear the noise of Saturday night closing at the pub on the next corner. Then, she thought, she would have to give it to him straight. Not just about the differences in their interests and lifestyles, but he also had to understand that she wasn't looking for anything permanent in her life.

Yet she hated the thought of hurting him.

'So just let me figure that out again. You're ten today, right?'

His grandson's squeal of laughter reached Fraser down the line. 'You can't count! I'm five. F-I-V-E.'

'Well, that's a relief. I was thinking you were double figures already.'

Fraser teased the boy a little longer, then, wishing him happy birthday again, asked to be put back to his mother.

'He loved the little tool set, Dad.' Joy resumed control of the receiver. 'Might be able to shame his father into doing something more around the place now.'

They chatted for a few moments longer until Fraser finally got around to what was on his mind. 'Love, I was wondering . . . Is there any chance you could get down here sometime? There's — well, there's someone I'd like you to meet.'

Joy stiffened. She saw at once that things were every bit as serious as Del had suggested. The time had come to confront the issue head on.

Now it was only a matter of settling on a date that suited them both.

With Joy agreeing to manage a visit, Fraser was left to arrange things with Maddy. Too excited to wait, he took the step of calling her in Sydney two nights later.

When she finally understood the purpose of the call Maddy took a deep breath. '. . . Meet your daughter? Fraser, I —'

'I've been itching to tell Joy about us, Maddy. But in the end I thought it best if she came down here and met you. She's got the kids to arrange of course but if you want to pick a weekend we could work it out to suit.'

It was then Maddy knew that her affair with Fraser O'Neill would have to end.

The early model Mercedes followed the Saab down the driveway to the cottage. Waving a hand out of the driver window Maddy indicated that her guests should park close to the front steps. That would make it easier for Neville.

'Maddy! It's wonderful!' Luke Allen slammed the car door behind him and stared admiringly at the sharply pitched metal roof with its attic windows, the deep shady verandah and comfortable wicker furniture. 'No wonder we couldn't find you most weekends.'

He leaned in at the car window and addressed the gaunt-looking man in the passenger seat. 'Isn't it great Nev?' Luke injected his tone with enthusiasm. 'Isn't Maddy a doll to share this with us?'

As Neville Tobin weakly agreed, Maddy felt a spasm of guilt. Her offer of the cottage as a retreat was well intentioned, but not without another motive.

For she hoped that the presence of the two friends would help to break the routine that had developed between Fraser and herself. Allow her to step back. Indicate to Fraser that things couldn't go on as he appeared to be hoping.

'Okay, guys, let me show you around.' Maddy climbed the steps to the front door while Luke helped his ailing friend from the car.

From the middle of the row of vines where he was supervising his contract pickers, Fraser saw in the distance not one, but two cars flashing through the trees that lined the drive to the old cottage.

His blue eyes narrowed under the stained brim of his hat. When he'd told Maddy that Joy was able to make it this weekend she'd vaguely agreed to try to get away. Now she had turned up, but had brought someone along with her. Fraser felt heavy with disappointment. He'd been looking forward so much to spending some time alone with her.

Then immediately he chastised himself. What the hell was he thinking about? If Maddy wanted to ask friends to stay that was her own business.

But as he turned back to his task he was filled with a sense of unease. Something was happening that he couldn't quite understand. The problem was, he thought, he'd had damn little experience of women like Maddy. Successful, self-assured, independent. All he knew was how he felt about her. And the sex, thrilling as it was, was only part of it. It had always been more, much more, than that. The feelings he had now were the same he'd experienced as a young man when he'd fallen so deeply in love with Nancy.

It had never occured to him that that same sort of passion and craziness could still affect you long after you'd gotten over being young.

After his shower that evening he wasn't sure what to do. It might be imposing just to drop in. Even to call.

And just as he was struggling to decide, the telephone rang.

It was her.

It was part of her strategy, to invite him over. Let him see her with her friends. Listen to their conversation. See for himself that their worlds were too far apart, that he could never fit in.

The gentlest solution.

While Kelly gave Maddy a joyous welcome, Fraser was taken aback to find himself in the company of two other males.

But it didn't take him too long to work things out.

As she handed Fraser a drink, Maddy explained. 'Luke and Neville are going to be staying at the cottage for a while, Fraser.'

He couldn't hide his surprise and Maddy added in vague explanation, 'It's a chance for them to get out of the city for a while.'

Taking a steadying sip of his drink, Fraser took in the young bloke's pale pinched face. And suddenly he suspected the reason behind Maddy's generosity. Holy hell . . . But then, he wrestled with his reaction, who was he to pass judgement on how other people lived their lives?

And if he was right about that bloke then Maddy was an even better human being than he'd imagined . . .

He smiled again at the two men sitting opposite. 'I'll say the same thing I said to Maddy then – give me a call if you need a hand with anything.'

'Thanks. Thanks a lot.' Luke Allen smiled politely although these days no one was capable of giving him the sort of help he really needed.

'We were just talking about the Harlem Dance Theatre,' Maddy continued, resuming her seat. 'Luke and Neville caught a performance when they were last in the States.'

'Amazing.' Neville Tobin managed to inject some of the enthusiasm he felt into his reply. 'Totally abstract. Music by Stravinsky and pure physical geometry from the dancers.'

Maddy was watching Fraser closely. But if she'd figured he'd be shocked by her choice of friends he showed no sign of it.

Over dinner, the conversation ranged from the latest avant garde theatrical production by a director they all knew, to a heated discussion about the worthiness of various Australia Council recipients, to the best hotel in Fiji.

As the talk flowed around him, Fraser listened quietly, pleased to learn something about the world that was so familiar to the woman he loved.

He felt no threat from Maddy's knowledge and expertise and his occasional question was put with no fear of revealing his ignorance.

'The only way to learn, isn't it?' he shrugged with a smile.

The evening passed pleasantly enough. Around midnight Maddy's houseguests indicated they were ready for bed and when goodnights were said, Fraser finally had Maddy to himself.

But to his disappointment she switched off the living room lights and walked him down the hall to the front door.

'Thanks for coming, Fraser. I hope we didn't bore you too much.'

He felt her cool quick kiss on his cheek but before he could hold her close she pulled away. Instead he reached for her hand and said softly, 'You know, Maddy, we can spend the night at my place if you'd prefer.'

She looked at him, and her voice when she spoke was very cool. 'Fraser, what's between us is private. Let's keep it that way.'

In the silence that followed Fraser stared back at her and Maddy felt her cheeks turn warm. Oh, God, why did it have to be so awkward. She didn't want to hurt him . . .

'I know what you're trying to do,' he said at last, his voice warm and low. 'I understand why these blokes are here. It's not easy for you, is it? Trusting someone, admitting to that need again?'

Her eyes held his for a long moment before she said a quiet goodnight.

Still dressed, Joy lay dozing on top of the bedcovers. She'd been half listening for the sound of her father's return and woke up at once when Fraser switched on the bedroom light.

'Joy! What in the world . . . Why didn't you let me know you were coming tonight?' He had seen her Toyota parked at the side of the house.

'Thought I'd surprise you, Dad.' Yawning, his daughter swung her long tanned legs off the bed.

If anything it was Joy who was surprised at her father's early return. Del had told her the woman was around most weekends so Joy'd been certain she'd catch him out when he returned in the early hours of the morning.

Fraser's recent telephone call had made it clear she should have tried to get down here before this. Things were even more serious than she had supposed and she wasn't going to let it ride a moment longer.

'Want a cup of tea, love?'

Joy shook her head and yawned widely again. 'I'm fine Dad.'

'You're tired. I'm glad you're here but we'll talk tomorrow, eh?'

'Sure. Goodnight, Dad.'

The snap of the switch, and Joy lay back in the darkness listening to his footsteps and the click of Girlie's claws retreating down the hall.

Tomorrow she would confront this head on. No way was she about to let her father make a fool of himself with some pushy city bitch who was just out for a good time.

CHAPTER FOURTEEN

Following their usual weekend routine Fraser had left Kelly behind with Maddy. Now the dog was her devoted shadow as she moved around the kitchen preparing breakfast.

Not that Maddy felt like eating anything herself. She hadn't slept well, unable to forget the hurt she had seen on Fraser's face. As she poured boiling water over freshly ground coffee, she hated herself for her bloody awful snobbery. Fraser was too good a man to be treated like that.

The trouble is, she told herself, she should never have got involved. She'd been independent for far too long to let any man into her life.

Absentmindedly she pushed down the coffee plunger. Well, now there was only one way to handle this. Up front. Tell him exactly how it was. She wasn't dealing with a child. Fraser was an intelligent man. He'd understand. After all it had only been a few months. He wasn't about to fall apart.

'You guys okay if I pop out for a while?' Keys in hand, eyes hidden behind dark glasses, Maddy emerged from the house with Kelly at her heels. Her visitors were still sipping coffee on the front verandah.

'Sure, Maddy,' Neville Tobin grinned. 'If any snakes drop in we'll tell them you won't be a moment.'

Maddy shook her head in mock disgust. 'Cit-ee boys.'

Fraser had also spent a restless, troubled night.

Lying in the single-man lane of his double bed he replayed Maddy's insinuation over and over in his head. That he couldn't fit in with her city life and friends. Of course he realised she had another life in Sydney. Different interests, different friends. But as exciting as she sometimes made it sound, he also sensed that it wasn't enough to fulfil her the way a woman like Maddy needed to be fulfilled. Despite their differences, he'd felt sure they had each found that elusive final element in the other that made them complete.

She's afraid, he told himself. She's spun a co-coon to keep herself safe and has forgotten how it feels to trust and let herself go.

Fraser knew it was up to him to prove that she had nothing to fear. And that it didn't matter a damn what other people thought.

'You going out, Dad?' Sipping at her third cup of tea Joy watched from the kitchen table as her father, foot on a chair, laced on his workboots.

'Yeah. Got some work to do on the garden at the back of the cottage. Want to make sure that water system is doing what it's supposed to.'

Joy's eyes hardened. 'From what I hear you're spending a lot of time over there.'

Something in his daughter's tone of voice made Fraser stop what he was doing and look up. 'Can't stop people talking, love.'

Sharply Joy cut across him. 'What's that woman want from you, Dad? Is it because you're handy to have around in more ways than one? Are you happy letting her use you like that?'

'Just a moment, Joy,' Fraser placed both feet on the floor and his voice was quiet and firm. 'Let's get something straight here. No one is using anyone in this relationship.'

'Relationship!' Joy shook her head in angry frustration. 'Oh, come on, Dad, you can't be serious!'

It wasn't the way Fraser had planned to bring up the subject of his feelings for Maddy. 'Love,' he said placatingly, 'you don't understand. A man's not dead till he's buried. What started as a friendship has gone much further than that now and Maddy Tyler is very special to me. That's why I asked you –'

Eyes blazing, Joy interrupted, her response carrying all the sting of a whiplash. 'And what are you going to do when she's had enough and laughs in your face, Dad? Can't you see you're nothing more to a woman like that than her bit on the side! Don't you know what people are saying!'

Fraser's hurt blue eyes met his daughter's furious gaze. But before either could speak, Girlie's barking announced a visitor.

'Joy, this is Maddy Tyler. Remember I told you? She bought the cottage from the Lancasters.'

Maddy greeted the unsmiling, dark-haired young woman, noting her resemblance to the photograph on the chiffonier. At the same time too she sensed the tension that filled the room. It seemed she'd picked a bad time to drop in. In any case with his daughter here it wasn't going to be possible to talk to Fraser. She'd have to leave it till another time.

Joy's cold, dark eyes studied the woman who was her father's lover. The expensive label jeans, the simple but elegant shirt with the fancy buttons, the gold hoops at her ears. An angry flush crept over her cheeks and her breath choked in her throat. This wasn't the sort of woman who would be interested in her father! Maddy Tyler was using him, making a fool –

The honk of a horn. Girlie's furious barking. Fraser, distracted, said, 'That must be Sam. He's looking for a piece to fix his generator. Make Maddy a cup of something, Joy. I'll just be a sec.' And he pushed his way through the screen door.

There was a moment's silence and considering the purpose of her visit, Maddy felt awkward at being left alone with Fraser's daughter. 'Perhaps, I should come ba –'

'What do you want with my father?' The attack was as blunt and direct as it was unexpected.

Maddy froze. The younger woman was staring at her tight-faced, her tension clear as she twisted the thin tea-towel in her strong brown fingers. So someone had told her. And she didn't like it.

'I really don't –' But again Maddy was interrupted.

Joy spat out her warning. 'I'm telling you – keep away from Dad!'

The irony of the situation was not lost on Maddy. Speaking calmly she said, 'I think I'd better come and see your father later.' Turning, she made for the door.

But the younger woman moved quickly, barring her way. 'You listen to me! My father had a terrible time when Mum died. They adored each other. You'll never care about him like that! And I'm not going to stand by and see him made a fool –'

'Joy!' Fraser stood white-faced in the doorway, the screen door breathing to a close behind him. His shocked expression revealed he had heard his daughter's angry words.

Shaken, he made a move towards Maddy. 'Maddy. Please. I'm so sor –'

She shook her head. 'No, Fraser, your daughter's right. It's exactly what I came to talk to you about. Not that it was meant to happen like this. And I'm sorry that it has. But you've got to understand, there's no future for us. I can't give you what you're looking for. We're too different, can't you see that? It was never meant to be.'

His blue eyes stared at her in shock. But Maddy didn't want to prolong the agony – for either of them. Turning on her heel, she pushed past the younger woman and headed down the hall.

Fraser's breath was rasping in his throat. He felt as if someone was tightening a noose around his neck. Gathering his wits, he ran after her.

'Maddy!'

She was already opening the door of her car but he grabbed her arm. 'Maddy. Please. This is crazy! You know what we have together is special. No matter how different our lives. Why don't you tell me what you're really running away from?'

Shrugging off his hold she turned to face him. 'Fraser, there's no reason to discuss it any further. Believe me, I'm sorry it's all happened this way but it was never going to be something that went on for ever. I wasn't looking for that, don't you understand? That's not what I need in my life.'

The pain in his eyes made her turn away. But better short-lived pain, Maddy consoled herself, than an ache that never went away . . .

Sliding behind the steering wheel, she fumbled with shaky fingers to fit the key into the lock.

Fraser leaned in at the open window gripping the top of the door with both hands. He spoke softly. 'When are you going to start being honest with yourself, Maddy? Admit that you're not that different from everybody else. That you need someone too. Stop making excuses, Maddy. Do you really want to waste the rest of your life mourning for a husband who's been dead almost twenty years?'

She gave him a long intense look, then the engine fired and she was gone.

CHAPTER FIFTEEN

Her city armour was back in place. The too glossy sheen on too tight lips. The salon sharp nails on tense, thin fingers. The designer clothes that shrieked forty-something, successful, street smart.

But Maddy Tyler hadn't been smart enough. And the secret inner doors had swung open, releasing a flood of remembered emotions. Anger. Guilt. Fear. Pain. Need . . .

I don't need Fraser O'Neill. She repeated the mantra as the clock ticked off the rest of her life. I don't need anyone.

Neville and Luke were delighted at the chance to stay at the cottage for a longer period. Neville still managed to paint, while Luke, a contributor to various gay publications, could write anywhere.

Maddy had told them the cottage was theirs at least through the winter. After that she'd put it on the market. For it hadn't taken her long to decide that that was the easiest solution. The least embarrassing and painful for both Fraser and herself. It was impossible to continue as neighbours after the way things had ended between them.

Maddy still hated herself when she remembered the terrible expression of hurt on his face . . . The words had come out all wrong. Made her sound hard and unfeeling. If the daughter hadn't been there, provoking the confrontation, she would have . . .

Oh, come off it, Maddy, a voice whispered somewhere inside her, you know there was no way of avoiding the issue. And honesty is always brutal . . .

Yet she tried to balance the guilt that churned inside her. Fraser, she told herself, had no right to make any comment on her feelings for Alex. He hadn't known her then. Only she knew how it had been. And no one, not even Fraser with his own sad history, could tell her how she should feel about that.

It was in such a state of mind that Maddy knew she had no choice but to remove the possibility of ever seeing him again.

So, sell up. Make money. Move on. A worthy representative of the generation that understood the real estate equation.

She had left her guests a list of what needed regular maintenance. 'I'm not sure if Fraser O'Neill will still be available. Maybe you could ask him. I'll forward his cheque as usual if he agrees.'

It was obvious that the two men had sensed there was something more behind the unexpected long-term offer of the house. But they were too polite to ask. Just as long, they said, as they 'weren't keeping her from using the place'.

Maddy had managed to pull out a laugh. 'Not at all. Done the country bit I think. Nearer next summer I'll put the place on the market.'

It was early March. And nothing moved in the winter.

People who knew her seemed smugly amused when they discovered she'd given up life 'at Greenacres'. 'A true city rat,' they grinned, 'is always going to miss the smell of heavy lead in the end.'

But as the next month slowly passed it was the smell of the earth Maddy missed. And the still, clear nights. The sight of heavy, ripening vines, the taste of newly-picked tomatoes, the gentle flap of bird wings overhead.

And when the sirens of the city's sentinels insisted on attention outside her windows at dawn, as the drunks and homeless shouted abuse from the nearby alleyways, Maddy sometimes found herself cursing Fraser. Why the hell had she let him cost her so much? Why hadn't she seen what was happening before it had come to this?

While Tony took a much needed break, Maddy threw herself back into work. Found new talent, chased buyers, did deals. But didn't entirely fall back into the old routine. She had long ago lost the desire to surround herself with the clamour of back-to-back, dress-up, see-and-be-seen social events. During the months at the cottage she had learned to enjoy her own company, had found her own calm centre.

Yet still there were nights when she'd remember the quiet, unobtrusive presence of the man who had presumed too much, come too close.

Those functions she did attend were almost exclusively connected with her work. At one of them she met a man. Fortyish, confident, flirtatious. Not particularly attractive but that hadn't mattered for a long time.

He chatted her up over drinks and sat next to her at dinner. His patter was practised and obvious but Maddy was bored and the game of seduction helped to pass the time.

Then, as they moved back into the sitting room for coffee, the door opened on a late arrival, a tall, toned graduate of the Elle or Cindy video. Young, blonde, potently aware of her effect. And Maddy saw her companion become instantly oblivious to the intellect, sophistication, and still-firm jawline of a woman his own age.

Yet she felt no resentment as she sat and sipped her cognac alone. She had learned a few years before that that was how things were going to be from now on. And she saw the blonde not as the enemy, but as mere cannon fodder.

Make the most of your decade, my darling, she silently transmitted. For after that invisibility descends. Or, if partnered, the terror of wondering when the hour of exile will arrive. When firmer, smoother flesh and young, burning eyes will prove too great a temptation for the package of testosterone that always needed more and more and more.

Fraser felt as if his insides had been scraped raw. His desire for her seemed to emanate from his flesh, surround him in an aura of palpable, painful need. He spent hours inside his head asking himself what sort of woman Maddy Tyler was.

He thought he had grown to know her. Had watched her slowly transformed – losing that brittle, cold edge, becoming warmer, more relaxed. Delighting in the same things that delighted him. Slowly he had dared to hope, and had fallen crazily, recklessly in love.

Why had she pushed him away? Because she really believed they were so different? Or was it the memory of her pain and loss that had made her withdraw and destroy, seal up her heart in her unrelenting urban bunker?

He tried ringing, three, four times. Hoping to convince her of the pointlessness of her fears. But the henchman of technology kept him at bay – the repetitive message of her clear, cool voice on the machine.

His only link was the cottage where her scent and presence still stirred, where his memory of those slow, warm nights pervaded the rooms.

'How's it going, Nev?'

The young man turned stiffly and smiled as his rural neighbour approached across the lawn.

'Not bad, Frase.' He was sitting with his easel under the shade of the pepper tree.

'Not disturbing you, am I?' Fraser moved closer, an open bottle of beer in his hand. He'd gotten into the habit of calling on Neville and Luke even without the excuse of having a job to do. To start with, it had been a chance to speak with those who knew Maddy in her other life, to tease out, casually, some detail that he didn't yet know. The clues that still might help him find a way through the checkpoints to her heart and soul.

But in the process he had seen at close hand another sort of love. Something that to begin with had seemed beyond his understanding but which, Fraser saw now, was capable of the same depth, and the same pain and fear of loss.

'You never disturb me, Frase.' Neville put down his brush and palette on the folding wooden table as Fraser squatted on the grass beside him.

It was true. There was something refreshing about this country bloke's company. His straight-forward, laid-back manner, the quiet humour that surfaced when you least expected it. And best of all, the overwhelming sense of solace and comfort he offered when, instead of avoiding the obvious subject, he encouraged Neville to talk about his fears and increasing panic about what lay ahead. It was an attitude far from the norm in the usual hetero Aussie male.

'What do you think of this?' Neville indicated the half-finished watercolour in front of him.

Leaning forward, Fraser squinted at the canvas which showed the front view of the cottage with both Girlie and Kelly sprawled out in the veran-dah shade.

His face split in a grin. 'Looks great – but you didn't get the models to take off their fur coats.'

'You got a thing about nudes, Frase?'

Fraser was glad to see the sudden sparkle that his gentle joke had brought to the young man's eyes. The deterioration was becoming more and more obvious and he couldn't help wondering if the painting on the easel would ever be finished.

For all the ways he tried to distract himself she was never out of his thoughts. In the end Fraser decided to write. But the struggle to put into words what was burning in his mind and heart and soul proved too much. Finally, he reduced it to a simple expression of his desire to meet and talk. 'Just give me a time, Maddy. I'll come to Sydney whenever you say.'

And then, the blade-edge torture of each passing hour as he waited for a reply.

The letter sat there for three days. On the fourth she rang his number. No niceties. No subtlety.

'Fraser, please, I don't want to hurt you any more than I have already. You took what happened between us far too seriously and now it's over. There's nothing to talk about. As soon as summer comes I'm putting the house on the market.'

A ring of ice numbed his lips and mouth, spread into his throat, almost choked him. 'But Maddy . . . what we had was precious. Don't you see that? Why can't —'

She stood at the baseline and served the killer. Cruel. Definite. Final. Hating herself. But the only way to end it once and for all.

'Fraser, your daughter understood what you refuse to see. We've got nothing in common. We never had. Except sex. But I'll find that somewhere else easily enough, and so will you.' She caught her breath, felt the stab in her soul as she flung the lie with brutal force.

'Maddy —' Her words pummelled him as painfully as fists.

But she hadn't finished. Last round. A knockout so he wouldn't get up. Wincing at her own savagery, but knowing she was saving him from the sharper, harsher, useless pain of drawn out longing. For Maddy knew how that felt. And it was something she would never risk again . . .

'What about Del? She's your type, isn't she? She's been damn patient enough. Fraser, face up to it, we both made a mistake. Get back to the life you belong in and leave me alone.'

Five minutes after hanging up she still sat stunned at her own ferocity. But at least he would hate her now.

And hate, she did her best to forgive herself, was the quickest path to healing.

'Thanks, Maddy. This is very good of you.' Jane's speech was distorted by the helmet of bandages encircling her swollen face.

'What are friends for if not to drive you home after your face lift?' Maddy smiled as she buckled herself in behind the wheel.

'Do you think I'm crazy?'

'Not as crazy as Cher.'

'Not yet.'

Carefully, Maddy pulled out of the hospital parking space and headed for the pay station. 'Listen, you don't need lines on your face to know you're wise.'

'You read that somewhere.' Jane turned her head away as Maddy lowered the window to pay the attendant.

'You're right. Some woman defending her surgery.'

Silence a moment as Maddy nosed out into the street and concentrated on finding an opening in the stream of homecoming traffic.

'Maddy, I'm so frightened! I don't want to be old!' There was a breathy tremor in Jane's voice. 'I still feel like a girl.'

'Rose Kennedy probably still felt like a girl.'

She kept it as light as possible, picking up the vibes of her friend's emotionally sensitive state. It wasn't every day, after all, that you had loose flesh sliced from your skull like pastry overhanging a pie dish.

'I want a man! I need someone to love me!'

Risking a sideways glance Maddy saw the tears welling out of those puffy bruised eyes.

She bit back the words she really wanted to say. You've got to love yourself, Jane. Rely on no one. *Needing* someone is a weakness. A threat.

Instead, she applied the balm of cliché, 'You'll be okay, Jane . . . We'll all be okay.'

Stiffly turning her neck, Jane looked at her from the wet, swollen promise of her freshly realigned man–catching face.

'How come you're so strong, Maddy?' It was more an accusation than a question. 'Why don't you need anyone? What makes you so damn self-sufficient!'

There was a long silence. Keeping her eyes on the traffic Maddy said with soft emphasis, 'It's taken me a long time to learn not to need anyone, Jane.'

But her body betrayed her. She had grown used to regular, blood-firing sex with a comfortable companion. Now she had to labour at closing her body down. Dousing the fire. Restraining herself once more in the straightjacket of celibacy. But it was like putting the genie back into the bottle.

Del knew all about the confrontation between Joy, her father and Maddy Tyler. And now she didn't intend wasting any more time. She had learned her lesson.

The news had got around about the new occupants of the cottage – 'shouldn't be allowed in the old O'Neill place' was the tight-lipped, local response. But what mattered to Del was that Maddy Tyler was no longer on the scene.

Early one evening she took the risk of calling on Fraser without warning. She found him surrounded by paper and files doing his bookwork at the kitchen table.

'Del . . .' Hiding his surprise he smiled a welcome. The dogs had given a warning bark, but before he could go out and investigate he'd heard the sound of heels tapping down the verandah. 'How've you been? Haven't seen you in an age.'

She moved past him into the room, aware as always of his effect on her. 'Could say the same myself, Fraser. Sorry to disturb you, just wondering how things are going.'

'Oh, can't complain, I guess. Take a seat. Want a cup of tea?'

There was a heaviness to his tone, and as he filled the kettle at the sink she saw that he'd lost weight. It etched a new haggardness on his face.

'New people in the cottage I hear.' She watched for his reaction.

'Yeah.'

'The Tyler woman not using it anymore?'

'Nope.'

Avoiding her eye, he placed a cup by her elbow and carried his own to the seat opposite.

'So you'll have a bit more spare time now then.'

'Maybe.'

They sipped in silence for a moment. Del had never known him like this. Brooding. Reluctant to talk. The dry humour nowhere in evidence.

She plunged in. 'Thought you might like to come to the club Friday night.'

The blue eyes moved to rest on her and Del found their dull opaqueness disturbing. She had the disquieting impression that Fraser was barely seeing her.

And then – 'Thanks, Del, but I guess I'll give it a miss this time.'

She weighed up the risks, but couldn't help herself. And anyway she hated seeing him like this. This wasn't the man she was used to.

She spoke quietly. 'You can't spend all your time brooding, Fraser.'

He shrugged, put down his empty cup on the tray beside him. 'Just don't feel like doing much socialising, Del.'

And then, in desperation, she unfurled her knowledge. 'It won't change anything you know, Fraser. Sitting here alone.'

He was aware that Joy and Del kept in occasional touch. Now he realised that Del knew what had happened.

'I'm okay, Del, no matter what anybody's said.'

Anxiety and anger sparked inside her. Burst into flame. 'How can you say that, Fraser? You're sitting here like some defeated old man! What have you let that woman do to you?'

'Del.' His voice held a warning note. 'I'd prefer not to talk about it, okay?'

She breathed deeply, berating herself for handling it so badly. Then, moving to his side she dropped to her knees by his chair, her concern beyond self-interest. 'Fraser, whatever happened, it's over. It wasn't right for you. I can't bear to see you like this.'

He stiffened and she almost winced at the look of pure pain she saw reflected in his eyes. Her heart went out to him and instinctively her hand moved to his knee in a gesture of comfort and compassion.

'Look, why don't you say you'll come on Friday? Try to get back into the swing of things. It'll be better for you than sitting here alone.'

For a long interminable moment he held her gaze. Then he gave a slight nod and with a weak smile covered her hand with his. 'Maybe you're right, Del.'

And her heart leapt.

CHAPTER SIXTEEN

Tony had worked with her too long not to know when something was wrong. But he also knew better than to ask. Maddy, he had found, moved in some invisible metallic field that kept real intimacy at bay.

Yet he recognised the changes. The forgetfulness, the occasional too-sharp response, the slight but apparent lessening of her usual high octane energy. Not to mention the abrupt change to her former weekend routine.

Still, she took him by surprise when she mentioned what she had in mind.

'You want to *move*? But, Maddy, Surry Hills is –'

'I don't mean the gallery. I'm talking about a place for me. Separate from work. My own place.'

They were having an after-work drink at one of the local gentrified pubs where the clientele were a demographically correct blend of Italian wool, black leather, and ripped denim.

'But isn't the cottage –'

'I'm talking more than just weekends,' abruptly she cut across him. 'Anyway, come summer I'm putting the cottage on the market. It's time I had a proper house in town.'

'Eastern Suburbs you mean?' said Tony.

Maddy shook her head. She wasn't after some inner-city fancy address where the neighbours didn't talk to you and their kids parked the Porsche across your driveway.

'No. I've started looking around the Northern Beaches. It'll be closer to my mother too.'

Tony Rabin couldn't hide his surprise.

To Maddy the plan seemed like a perfect compromise. She missed the cottage but it could only ever have been a weekend escape. Now she wanted to find a home within driving distance of the gallery yet in the sort of environment that might offer a similar harmony with nature.

She started doing the rounds of real estate offices and, if her search was not immediately promising, it at least helped to fill weekends that had suddenly grown so empty.

The Peninsula lay about an hour's drive north of the city, and its forested hillsides looked east to the Pacific. If she was lucky enough she might even find a place that also took in the marinas and waterways of the Pittwater inlet to the west. Not that she was kidding herself that the area was cheap, but with what she would get for the cottage, plus a mortgage on the gallery, she could just do it.

And then Fate played Maddy Tyler one of its famous double aces.

'It sounds *wonderful*, Jeff! Just what I'm looking for. When can I see it?'

They drove up the next afternoon. Jeff Overton was a successful television producer and Maddy had known him and his wife for almost ten years. When she'd mentioned her search Jeff had thought at once of the perfect property.

'It belongs to one of my top writers. He's finding more and more work for himself in the States these days and I know he's very seriously considering putting the place on the market. Leaving a house with a large garden is always a problem. Bob knows he'd be better off with an apartment in the city.'

'You mean it isn't definitely on the market?' They were winding up a steep road under the peeling branches of eucalypts.

'He just needs the right buyer to convince him.'

The house sat at the top of a steep driveway at the end of a cul de sac. For Maddy it was true, clichéd love at first sight. The long, low sandstone building was less than twenty years old but looked as if it had been there forever. Ivy grew on its external walls, shutters edged the cedar french doors and the pergola was shaded by a vigorous rambling rose.

Though high enough to offer glimpses of the ocean through the trees, the house stood on enough level ground to be surrounded by established lawns and gardens. 'It's magical,' Maddy breathed, as she caught sight of a kookaburra drinking at the terracotta fountain beneath the broad shade of two enormous pines.

Bob McCall was a friendly, articulate man with a short dark beard and gold framed glasses. As he showed Maddy through the house she wondered how he could ever bear to leave the place. Less traditional inside than out, it had a variety of interesting ceiling heights and large areas of glass that made the most of the views. A covered walkway led to a small, self-contained guest cottage.

'We can hardly bear to leave it,' Anne McCall echoed Maddy's thoughts afterwards as she offered afternoon tea. 'But it's just become more and more impractical for our lifestyle.'

With a directness shaped by the years, Maddy came straight to the point. 'Is it for sale or not?'

As it turned out, the arrangement suited everyone. The McCalls were leaving for LA later that month and would be away for the rest of the year. During that time they would finally make up their minds what to do. Meanwhile, Maddy could rent the house with first option to purchase if they made the decision to sell.

'I'm sure you'll get it, Maddy.' Jeff spoke confidently as they drove back to town. 'Bob's career is taking off like a rocket. It's just not practical to hang onto a place like that.'

That was how Maddy had read it too. And the good thing about the few months leeway was that it gave her plenty of time to sell the cottage and have the money in hand.

But the second throw of the dice was yet to come.

Her examination over, Maddy re-dressed and went back into her doctor's consulting room.

'Take a seat, Maddy.'

As the time had passed since her attack she had stopped being afraid. It was three months since her last check-up and, apart from feeling a little more tired than usual, Maddy was certain everything would be normal.

And then her life turned upside down.

'Maddy, do you have any reason to suspect you might be pregnant?'

The next morning's test proved positive. The doctor's guess was three months.

He looked at her white face across the desk. 'You're almost forty-three, Maddy. How do you feel about having a baby?'

Just at that moment Maddy Tyler didn't know whether she wanted to laugh or cry.

Maddy the decisive. The controlled. The capable.

And now she could barely operate as she tried to comprehend life's latest punch to her solar plexus.

She hadn't given contraception a thought. Her periods had grown scantier and more erratic over the last couple of years and even more so during her illness and recovery. A woman of her age wasn't meant to be fertile!

'We'll need a quick decision, Maddy.' The doctor had made that clear. 'If you decide to keep it we'll do the tests needed for a woman your age.'

For two days and nights a stream of repetitive thoughts ran through her mind like the high-tech news headlines in Times Square.

A baby . . . Fraser's baby . . . At forty-two . . .

As the years had passed and the possibility of finding someone and settling down had gradually disappeared Maddy had come to accept the painful reality that she would never have a child of her own. Conceiving without love had never been an option – though she would never condemn those who chose that particular path.

But now, suddenly, totally unexpectedly, with the door to motherhood about to clang shut behind her – an eleventh hour reprieve. A final chance that left her reeling with disbelief.

That it should happen at this stage of her life – when she was successful, independent, free. Running her own show. And ready in three days time to move into a new home.

During the next two days and nights memories of Alex and that first abortion tormented her incessantly. She thought of the child she had destroyed. Of the soft, plump arms that had never slipped around her neck, of the pink cherub mouth she had never kissed, the long-lashed eyes she had never seen closed against a life-fresh cheek.

Oh, Jesus. Oh dear Jesus . . .

At the same time she pondered too the difficulties of single motherhood. The caked and stinking nappies. The milky vomit and sprayed food. The endless sleepless nights and siren screams. She thought of schools and schedules, money and fees, adolescent tantrums, drugs, and lack of freedom.

And finally she thought of Fraser.

Oh, Maddy, Maddy, what are you going to do?

'I'm having it.' Dressed in a cherry-red suit she sat tensely facing the doctor across his desk.

He raised a professional eyebrow. 'Then we'd better get you an obstetrician and have all the necessary tests done at once.'

She was glad of the distraction of the move. It stopped her thinking of the outcome of all the medical fuss of ultrasounds and blood tests and guessed-at dates. For now, having made the most momentous decision of her life, Maddy felt imbued with an incredible spirit of joy and anticipation and excitement. It filled her heart and soul, warmed her blood and glowed upon her flesh.

That first night in the house on the hill she went out into the garden and stood on the moonlit lawn imagining her future.

Her son or daughter sleeping beside her in the shade of the pram, learning to crawl on this green, springy lawn, running into her arms with squeals of pleasure when she came home from work.

Tears welled in her eyes and in the cool night air Maddy Tyler cried for the children she had wrenched unripened from her womb, and for the one to whom she would now give everything in an attempt to make amends.

She thought a lot about what Fraser might do if he found out. Would he try to interfere? These days there were men who chose to assert their claim to fatherhood rather than deny it. Who chased their lovers through the courts, fighting for their rights. Not that she thought Fraser likely to do that, but you never knew.

No, Maddy was fiercely determined, this baby was hers. And she didn't need anybody else's money or time or input to bring it up.

Yet, the thought often swam into her consciousness, if the child had inherited its father's gentle serenity and goodness of heart she wouldn't mind at all . . .

She came to terms too about worrying what her friends might say. A two day wonder. Gossip and speculation, then they'd all be too busy planning their next career moves, making their next real estate killing, to give much thought to Maddy Tyler, older mother to be.

'At your age it's a bit more of a lottery, Ms Tyler.'

It was early morning a few days later. She was dressed and ready for work when her obstetrician's secretary rang through with the results. 'And I'm happy to say you've won. All the tests are normal.'

Her lips trembled. She couldn't reply. Dropping the receiver she covered her face with shaking fingers as tears of joy and relief tracked through her freshly applied make-up.

For the first time in years Maddy Tyler had found a reason to look forward to the future.

CHAPTER SEVENTEEN

'You sure you don't want to come in?'

Fraser had walked her to the front door and even though Del knew there wasn't much hope, she felt she had to try.

'I don't think so, Del. But I enjoyed myself tonight. Thanks again for asking me.'

She heard the hollowness in his tone which belied the polite words. This was only the second time she'd managed to coax him to the club but the night had been no more successful than the first.

Oh, he'd tried, she could see that. But as the evening wore on, and the others around the table let their hair down, she'd watched Fraser withdraw more and more into himself.

She'd tried to jolly him up, even managed to get him on his feet once to dance, but it was painfully clear, to her at least, that Fraser's heart was not in socialising.

'Goodnight then, Fraser.' She stretched up and gave him a kiss on the cheek, at the same time squeezing his hand. She couldn't make the message more obvious than that.

'If you want company, you know where I am,' she said softly as he turned to go.

'You're a good friend, Del. Thanks.'

The moonlight was bright enough for her to watch him walk to the pick-up. His whole body was heavy with despair.

When was he going to snap out of it, she wondered. She would never have believed it could affect him so badly or so long.

And Del Bradley cared enough for Fraser O'Neill to wonder if perhaps she and Joy should never have interfered. Things might have been different if the affair had just been allowed to run its course.

Maddy woke each morning with the buzz of happiness in her veins. She'd never felt so content. She ate well, slept well, looked forward to her regular obstetric appointments. And when the ultrasound revealed she was going to have a daughter she laughed aloud with joy. Each day, each hour that passed brought her closer to the moment when she would hold this miracle in her arms.

It was now she began to recognise a wider pattern in her life. Felt the utter certainty that we each have a route marked out for us, a map we are allotted at our births. She now saw a purpose in her time at the cottage, accepted that as part of the blueprint of her life she had been meant to meet Fraser O'Neill. To fall pregnant and have the child who now stirred in her belly.

But as the weeks passed Maddy was forced to consider what it meant to deny Fraser his child. And the child a father. But she couldn't allow herself to dwell on that. A relationship with Fraser was still out of the question. One day, perhaps, the time would be right and she would speak to her daughter about her father. About his strength and honesty, his generosity and humour. About those few short months that had given her life.

But in the meantime, Maddy determined, this child was hers. She would bring her up alone.

As she had done so much in her life alone.

The gossip grew as surely as her belly. There was plenty of speculation about the identity of the father, and few of those who guessed kept the knowledge to themselves. Yet none was blunt enough to say anything to Maddy's face.

Except Jane.

'Are you going to tell him, Maddy?'

They were having lunch in a small brasserie not far from the gallery. Inside, not in the courtyard, where the sun might have threatened Jane's expensive face.

'There's no need to.'

Jane heard the finality in Maddy's voice. 'What if he finds out?'

'Not a chance.'

'Someone might tell Luke or Neville.'

She'd considered that, but had pushed the thought out of her mind. 'People tend to lose touch when they learn about the plague, Jane. Hadn't you noticed?'

Maddy felt her friend's gaze as she wound pasta around her fork. Then Jane said softly, 'There's been a lot of gossip as you can imagine, Maddy. People love a good scandal. But if you need me all you have to do is pick up the phone.'

Her voice reflected her genuine kindness and concern and Maddy reached across the table and covered her friend's hand with her own. The bond of sisterhood.

'Thanks. I'll always remember you said that.'

Maddy wasn't going to let herself be troubled by the gossip. Let people say what they liked. Nothing could diminish her happiness, and her serenity transcended everything.

With quiet assurance she moved through the stages of her pregnancy. Wearing simple, elegant maternity shifts in fine wool she ran the gallery, and at home she finished decorating the nursery. Her life was completely full.

The move to the Northern Beaches had brought her nearer to the nursing home and she was able to visit her mother more regularly. But it still pained her sharply that she had no way of sharing her exciting news with the frail, silent woman who stared at her through blank blue eyes.

And then, late one Saturday afternoon, the telephone rang with the news that her mother had passed away. Peacefully. In her sleep. Or did they always tell you that?

As Maddy listened to the professional sympathy of the matron she experienced a succession of emotions. Grief, regret, relief. When she hung up she wept for the mother she had lost long before.

The funeral was a brief, sad affair, and as she stood in the sunshine and watched the coffin being slotted into the neat, red slice of earth, Maddy was hit by a sense of truly overwhelming aloneness. For despite her mother's illness there had always been the knowledge that someone still breathed who shared her blood, who linked her to her childhood and the past. Now nothing stood between Maddy and her own mortality.

Fraser heard the barking and came out to investigate. It was the sort of shrill, excited sound that told him the dogs had something bailed up.

It was dusk, the air turning cold, but he could see them in the paddock, front legs stretched out, backsides up, tails flagging rigidly. They took no notice of his calls and whistles.

Fraser frowned. Couldn't be a snake. Not at this time of the year. But he picked up his shot-gun anyway before heading out the door.

As he moved closer the dogs didn't lose their concentration on whatever was exciting them. Kelly was the more frantic, circling tightly, her bark high-pitched, her eyes never leaving what-ever so closely held her attention.

And then Fraser saw it. A king brown. Lethal. Ready to strike.

'Girlie! . . . Kelly! *Here!*' Fraser raised his gun. But he couldn't fire while the dogs were in his way.

The snake lashed out. The younger dog was the quickest. And as Kelly leapt clear it was Girlie who took the sharp sting of those venomous fangs.

A terrible yelp. Another. Then Fraser blasted with the gun.

It was over by the time he got her to the vet.

'I'm sorry, Fraser.' The man helped him to lay the still warm body in the back of the pick-up. He knew how it felt to lose a friend. 'Sometimes those king browns hang around long after the heat's gone out of the sun.'

Fraser drove home, and alone in the dark dug Girlie's grave.

'Oh, Bob, that's wonderful! I'm delighted. I really love the place. And we can settle in the New Year you say? That's perfect.'

The phone call brought the news Maddy had been waiting for. The McCalls were going to sell. The house would be hers. The lawyers would make it legal and binding and she'd still have time to sell the cottage before settlement.

A couple of days later she rang Neville and Luke with the news.

'. . . there's no need to rush away though, Luke. It's Neville I'm thinking of. The place won't sell that quickly, I'm sure.'

'That's kind of you, Maddy, but the way things are we may have to move back to town sooner than we thought.'

She caught her breath, knew at once what he meant. 'Is it –?'

'Yes . . . Took him down for his check-up last week. It's – it's not looking good.'

She heard the careful control in his voice. 'Oh, God, Luke . . . I'm so sorry. You know if there's anything at all I can do –'

'Thanks. But nobody can do anything. That's the rules of this game.' His tremulous breath reached her down the line. 'But I want you to know, Maddy, that the time we've had here's been precious for us. Really precious.'

'I'm glad about that, Luke.'

'In fact one of the best tonics for Nev has been Fraser. Could've given us the cold shoulder, just done his work and shot through. But he figured out what was going on. He'd hang around yarning with Nev and let him talk about things in a way he avoids with me. A real good bloke. But I guess you got to know him quite well.'

'I – we were friendly. No big deal.'

'Well he always took the time to ask about you.'

Maddy made no comment but Luke didn't seem to notice.

'A real pity about his dog.'

'Dog? What dog?' Maddy's voice rose. 'What happened?'

'The big one. Girlie. Bought it with a snake. If you ask me it really broke the bloke apart.'

For a long time after she had hung up Maddy felt an enormous weight of sadness and emptiness she didn't really understand.

Fraser sat on the faded sofa and stared into the crackling fire. Beside him, Kelly stretched out with her slim pretty head in his lap, her eyes not closed but watching him as she listened to his voice.

'I got you for her, Kel, and now you're all I've got for me.' Fraser spoke softly as he rhythmically stroked the dog's thickening coat.

Oh, Jesus . . .

Dropping his head back against the sofa, he squeezed his eyes shut. He was too damn old for self-pity! Get your act together, Fraser. She's gone, it's over!

Girlie's death had only made things worse and now Del was really concerned. Concerned enough to put another call through to Joy.

'I'm worried about him, Joy. This has gone on too long. And Girlie's death didn't help. I was thinking it might be a good idea if he got away for a while. Came to stay with you and the boys. What do you think?'

At the other end of the line Joy felt the twin burdens of worry and guilt. Del had called her once before about her father's state of mind. And now Joy was forced to admit that maybe the older woman was right. Perhaps they should have left well enough alone. Let things run their course.

But, she did her best to soothe her conscience, her father would get over it in time. He had to. Because as Maddy Tyler had made abundantly clear – she had never wanted him as he had wanted her.

CHAPTER EIGHTEEN

As she entered the sixth month of her pregnancy Maddy began to prepare for her life following the baby's birth.

Over the first few months at least she intended to cut back even more sharply on her working hours. As she spent time with Tony planning forthcoming projects Maddy knew how fortunate she was to be able to depend on his experience and skill.

Even so, she still surprised herself at the ease with which she was able to relinquish her once substantial power and control. Being in charge had been her way of life for so long. But now so much had changed.

For even later when, with the help of a part-time nanny, she would resume some of her former responsibilities, Maddy still had no intention of allowing work to consume too much of her precious time.

She had a child to consider now. Her late-life miracle.

And so Maddy Tyler made her plans. Those dazzling temptations to Fate. And like so many of us she succumbed to the folly of believing that life would work out exactly as she had it plotted.

'It's nothing to get too worried about yet but at your age we can't take chances.' The obstetrician's professionally soothing tones always seemed to Maddy to err on the side of paternal condescension. 'I think it might be best that we admit you – just to keep an eye on everything. Bed rest should be enough to put things right.'

But of course Maddy worried. By now she had read enough of the relevant literature to know that her fluctuating high blood pressure and peripheral swelling were the forerunners to toxemia. Something that could put both her child and herself at risk.

In the plush private hospital she felt like an interloper – a mother who yet wasn't – among other legitimate females who were there to give birth. Alternately bored and anxious she grilled each staff member suspiciously whenever they appeared with their clipboards and orders and evasive expressions.

Then, after eight days of careful monitoring, both her blood pressure and anxiety were sufficiently reduced to enable her grateful escape and it was a solicitous Jane who drove her home.

'Remember what Sophia Loren went through?' Jane offered rather obliquely. 'Months of total bed rest. And she was ten years younger than you. You've got to keep taking it easy, Maddy.'

Maddy looked out at the misty drizzle of a winter's day and with her newly restored confidence in the experts answered calmly, 'Medical science has come a long way since then, Jane. This baby is going to be fine.'

'I'm sure you're right. I just wish I wasn't going to be in London when you're due.'

'Believe me, six months in the London office is a much better deal I'm sure than six hours of listening to me moaning in childbirth.' Maddy spoke lightly, but she would miss Jane's support.

Taking her eyes off the traffic, her friend shot her a quick glance. '*Six* hours? Are you kidding? Try thirty-six, darling. And if you're as stoic as I was you'll be screaming like a banshee all the way.'

She was mesmerised by her changing body. The soft, swollen incubator of a new life. Her breasts continued to bloom as she watched. Pale, full globes traced with blue, heavying themselves in preparation for tiny, limpet lips.

As the life force fluttered inside her Maddy felt an intensity of emotion that threatened to break through her flesh. She realised now that over all the years as friends had fallen pregnant and given birth she had never really understood. Never, never, could she have imagined that it would feel like this.

The men had left the cottage and a bed was found for Neville in an inner-city hospice. Maddy visited when she could and Luke spent most of every day at his lover's side. So he was there that afternoon when one of the staff brought another visitor to the door.

Following Luke's look of surprise Neville painfully turned his head on the pillow. And his pale lips spread in a rare smile.

'Fraser!' Luke rose to his feet. Fraser O'Neill, dressed in moleskins and tweed jacket, and carrying a basket of fruit, quietly greeted the two men. As he approached the bed his height and presence seemed to fill the room.

'Just wanted to say g'day, Nev, see they were looking after you okay. I reckon Kelly really misses you blokes.'

And he reached out and gripped the dying man's outstretched hand.

As Fraser made his way out of the hospital car park for the long drive home the ache that never went away was sharpened by the knowledge that Maddy was so close yet no longer accessible.

The memory of what they'd shared was burnt into his mind and heart like the faulty frame of an old film reel. Nothing was the same now that she had touched and was gone from his life.

He had tried but been unable to penetrate the barriers and complexities of Maddy Tyler's past.

She called Luke regularly and whenever they spoke she could sense the sharpness of his pain.

Now into her eighth month, she still felt compelled to make the offer.

'Why don't you come up next weekend, Luke? Get away from it for a while? It'll do you good.'

He hesitated, but in the end let himself be persuaded. For Luke Allen too needed somewhere to cry and someone to offer comfort.

The days were warming and they sat in the afternoon sunshine by the wide picture window. In the distance lay the thin, blue ribbon of the Pacific.

Luke studied her as she poured their tea. 'It's true what they say, Maddy. You're blooming. Is everything going well?' The conventions of good manners. Before surrendering to the topic that obsessed him.

'Fine.'

It wasn't strictly true. Yesterday's check-up had revealed that her blood pressure was once more on the rise and Maddy could see for herself the frightening swelling in her fingers and legs. She recalled too the calm voice of the expert in whom she had placed her trust. 'If this doesn't go down over the weekend, call me. We might have to think about admitting you for the final weeks.'

She had left the consulting rooms feeling anxious and exhausted. It probably would have been better to put Luke off but she knew she couldn't do that.

She said now, 'Tell me about Neville.'

And amid quiet sobs he did.

At around five the next morning the pain awoke her from a restless sleep. For an hour longer she endured.

And then thanked God that Luke was there.

Time passed in molten moments as strangers moved in and out of the room. A kaleidoscope of sensory perception: the low beep of some machine, the rasp of starch against starch, the sting of needles, the touch of cool professional flesh.

And through it all the constant back beat of agonising pain.

At some point she was dimly aware of her obstetrician's face leaning close to hers. 'We're going to induce the baby, Maddy. You'll be fine.'

He stood beside her bed, the words flowing out of his mouth and over her head. '. . . a respiratory problem . . . keeping an eye on her . . . sure she'll be fine . . .'

Maddy smiled weakly, her eyes fluttering in exhaustion, her body feeling as if it had been dragged over metal spikes. But she smiled.

Because in a room at the end of the corridor her newborn daughter had become part of the world.

She was one of three babies in the nursery's intensive care.

They wheeled Maddy up to the humidicrib and she saw for the first time the tiny creature to whom she had given life. The pale almost transparent body barely bigger than a kitten's. The eggshell thin skull, the bracelet thin fingers.

And the tubes and drips that made her look like the smallest astronaut attached to the mother ship.

'If you put your finger in here you can touch her.' The sister had heard the longing in her blood.

Tears rolling down her cheeks, Maddy inserted her index finger into the single digit glove.

And at that moment, as she touched her future, her soul was shaken by a sudden vibration. The sense of Fraser's presence was almost over-whelming . . .

Luke sat by the bedside and held her hand. 'So that's how it works. I was meant to be with you this weekend.'

'The hand of God . . .?' Maddy gave him a weary smile.

'The hand of God,' he agreed.

Jane talked with her from London, her delight echoing down the line. 'See, they can't put us aged mares out to paddock yet, darling! Congratulations! I can't wait to see her.'

Tony and other friends came to visit and filled the room with flowers and gifts.

'What are you going to call her, Maddy?'

Maddy smiled. 'Francesca.'

Those who had never been able to swallow that other crazy rumour now decided the lover had been some wildly handsome Italian.

Ah yes, that was more like Maddy.

Two days later she held her baby for the first time.

And the last.

They left her alone and her tears fell on her dead daughter's paling, cooling skin. On her closed, silky eyes that would never now see the sun or the moon or the stars, or her growing beauty in the mirror, or her mother's aging face.

There was no one to blame. Unless Maddy wanted to blame Francesca herself for her impatient birth. And the toxemia that had left her underdeveloped, susceptible, prey to the infection that had killed her.

Why, God! Why?

Later, as she lay alone in the straitjacket of her hospital bed, the words screeched with agonising repetitiveness in Maddy's head. Why, when she had finally been offered the miracle cure for a broken heart, had it been torn away so soon? Why had she lost the one tiny being she could trust with her love?

And, appalled by her need, and despising her weakness, Maddy found herself longing for Fraser's calm strength and the comfort of his uncomplicated heart.

But it was far far too late for that.

CHAPTER NINETEEN

So few of us are able to speak openly of death. It is the natural end of our journey yet we shy from the knowledge that at the very moment of our birth our ticket awaits us.

After the tragedy of her daughter's death, some who knew Maddy felt compelled to keep their distance. Too sharp for them, the reminder of their only certain future. And then there were others who lacked the courage or ability to confront another human being's deepest pain.

But those closest to her, Tony, and Luke, and Jane – who had immediately flown home – did their best to help her through that traumatic time. It was Jane who sat with her night after sleepless night, holding her, letting her weep, knowing better than to offer empty words. And Luke too understood. For he had learned his own lessons about love and compassion, about feeling and sharing the searing pain of loss and displacement.

In time, Maddy's body recovered from the birth. But not her heart. Weeks passed and she remained inconsolable. For the first time in her forty-two years Maddy Tyler lacked the determination and drive that had always been her certain source for overcoming the setbacks of her life.

She was interested in nothing, would sit for hours staring at the same open page of a book or magazine, her eyes too big in her hollow cheeked face. And the torment of her loss never diminished.

Why? Why had she been left so alone? Why had she been cast so adrift from those she loved? Her father, her mother, her husband, and now her innocent baby daughter.

They were questions that could never be answered but Maddy never left them alone.

The weeks passed and she grew thinner and weaker, showed no interest in work and business that had always been her saviour in the past. And watching her, Jane knew she had to do something.

Megan Stewart was more than willing to help. Jane had worked as editor on the psychologist's best-selling book and the two women had remained friends. One afternoon Jane brought her to the house. Without bothering to clear it with Maddy. For she knew what the answer would have been.

They found her sitting in the garden. Absolutely still. Eyes empty as they stared at the distant sea. Body bent and frail. Jane made the introductions. 'Megan's a friend of mine, Maddy. I brought her here to meet you.'

Slowly Maddy lifted her eyes to focus on her visitor. She had no idea what this plain, grey-haired woman with the soft smile and kind eyes was doing in her garden.

'I'll go get us some tea,' Jane announced.

And Megan Stewart sat down beside the woman whose torment was so great she felt it reaching out to pierce her own flesh.

It took four visits. But when Maddy finally started to talk she spared Megan Stewart nothing. Her grief, her anger at a world that had robbed her of so much, her need for love, and her fear of it – and finally, the unresolved confusion of her feelings for the man she had thought so wrong for her.

'Fraser saw life so simply . . . It was *me*. I made things complicated! I told myself he could never be right for me. I needed a man who was cultivated, sophisticated, who understood art and music and books. Someone who could fit in with my friends, my lifestyle. But then . . . when I saw my baby for the first time it suddenly felt as if maybe I'd got it all *wrong*. With Fraser I did things and experienced things I'd never done before. Simple things . . . Magical things . . . Watched things grow, listened to the sun on the leaves, the rain on the roof. I used to feel as if Fraser could see into my soul. He knew I was lonely. He understood what that was like. And when I was with him I felt at peace. Comfortable. As if I could take a break from being this person who always had to be perfect and in charge and strong.'

Tears were running down her cheeks and she had no idea how painfully tight she was clutching the psychologist's hand. 'You were afraid, weren't you, Maddy?' Megan Stewart's voice was gentle. 'Because of Alex. You felt yourself falling for Fraser and you needed excuses.'

Maddy raised her stricken face to the woman who sat beside her. 'I couldn't bear the thought of hurting like that again. The only way was to never ever let anyone else get as close. But now . . .' her voice was choked with pain, 'I know I've made a terrible mistake. I let go of the best thing that's happened to me in years.'

Maddy was shocked by the sense of release the admission brought her. And now she began to talk openly about Fraser to Jane too. As if by talking she could bring the man she had lost back into reality.

'Oh, Maddy . . .' Jane hugged her with compassion, 'don't be so hard on yourself. Maybe at our age the real thing isn't easy to recognise. Especially when it doesn't come in the package we expect.'

Drawing back she looked into her friend's anguished face. 'Why don't you go and see him? Maybe if –'

'No!' Maddy's reaction was as violent as it was abrupt. 'Don't you see? He could never forgive me. I had his child and he never got a chance to see her . . .'

Luke was not really surprised to learn the identity of the child's father.

'Fraser O'Neill's one of those special people, Maddy. We were both lucky to know him. Even for a while.' His arm was around her shoulders and he was hugging her close. 'And you're not the only one to make a mistake. So many of us never know that we've had something very special until it's too late.'

She tried, at least, to pull herself together. She went back to the gallery but although Tony did his best to enthuse her, Maddy's heart wasn't it.

She knew too she would have to get serious now about ridding herself of the cottage. With Christmas a few short weeks away the market would soon start moving. But first she needed to make one last visit to the place to clear out what was left of her things.

Yet the thought of being so close to Fraser filled her with dread.

Luke spoke to Neville about what had happened. He was much weaker now but when life is short the mind sometimes becomes luminously focused.

It was early one Saturday morning that Luke drove out of Sydney on the trip north. The plainly wrapped package sat on the passenger seat beside him. He could do what he had to do and still be back with Neville by the afternoon.

'If you'd been three minutes later you'd have missed me.' Fraser pushed the sugar jar across the table to his one-time neighbour. He'd been heading down the drive on his way to help clear lantana on Keith Curlow's place when he'd come head to head with a car turning off the main road.

'Neville would have been upset if I had,' said Luke. And as he handed across the package he saw the older man's puzzled frown.

'He wanted you to have this, Fraser. A thank you. It could've . . . well, it could've waited till – afterwards, but he figured he'd like you to have it now.'

Carefully, as his unexpected visitor was talking, Fraser removed the string and wrapping paper to find a small framed painting. It was the one he had watched Neville working on that day under the pepper tree. The one which showed Girlie and Kelly together on the cottage verandah.

'I –' There was a shake in Fraser's voice and he started again. 'It's real good of him, Luke. It's something I'll really treasure. You tell him that for me, okay?'

Luke nodded and took a swallow of his coffee. There was a moment's silence then he took a breath and carefully embarked on the second reason for his visit.

'. . . and I guess you probably wouldn't have heard, but Maddy's had her own reason to grieve lately.'

Luke nodded as Fraser's eyes came to rest on his. 'Yes. It was terrible. She lost a baby. Two days old.'

Fraser felt a stone settle in the bottom of his belly. It still hurt like hell. 'I'm real sorry to hear that, Luke. But – I didn't know Maddy had married.'

'Oh she's not. No husband. Bit of a puzzle really. We're in regular contact and I know for a fact there's been no one in her life in the city.' He left a silence for that one to sink in.

Fraser's workworn hands were gripped around his empty coffee mug. 'When did all this happen?'

'About three months or so now. But it's still tearing her apart.' A beat. 'I've done all I could but it doesn't seem to be doing much good. You know, Fraser, I sometimes think if I only knew who the father was . . . and if he was, well, you know, the right type of bloke, I'd let him know what's happened. Maybe he's the only one now who can help her come through all this.'

CHAPTER TWENTY

She didn't have the courage to face going alone and asked Jane to come with her.

'I — it'd just be so difficult if I bumped into Fraser, Jane. I can only imagine what I've done to him and I couldn't bear to make it worse. For either of us.'

'Of course, Maddy. I'll do anything to help.'

But Jane had already talked to Luke. Late on the Friday afternoon when they were due to leave, Maddy received a phone call.

'I'm sorry, Maddy.' It was Jane. 'I'm laid up with the flu. Hit me out of nowhere. I've just come straight in the door and fallen into bed.' It was a lie. But as she replaced the receiver Jane knew she'd done the right thing.

Now Maddy might have the chance to explore the limits of her courage.

It felt as familiar as yesterday and yet as strange as if years had passed. As she bumped up the drive her headlights revealed how trees and shrubs and bushes had grown in her absence. The cycle of life, its rhythm indifferent to human tragedy.

Her heart was pounding as she climbed the front steps and used her torch to fit the key in the lock. The jasmine was in sweet bloom on the night air and it felt like a lifetime ago since she had first stepped under those heavy tresses.

The house was dusty but exactly as she remembered, and as she slowly moved from room to room Maddy felt something of the peace and ambience she remembered drift again into her bones. But now there was something more.

The walls around her seemed to breathe with the presence of Fraser. She sensed him everywhere. His spirit was in this house as surely as it had been in his newborn daughter. In this house that had been built by Francesca's great-grandfather . . .

A sob caught in her throat and she moved out to the verandah where she and Fraser had shared so many warm evenings. The wicker chairs had been stowed away and she sat down on the steps and stared into the darkness.

She remembered that first night when, like now, she'd sat in a pool of golden light and felt the magic of connection to something greater than herself. When some subtle shift had taken place inside her and her eyes had opened to the delight of pleasures so fresh and so different from everything she had known. Cool, deep creeks and star-full skies, dark earth and the morning call of

birds, firm new buds on sinuous trailing vines . . .
The simple beauty of life's very special gifts.

And yet, she railed at herself, squeezing her
eyes tight, the greatest gift of all she had failed to
recognise. The offer of love. Pure and uncon-
ditional. Simple and honest.

And now she would have to live the rest of her
life knowing she had lost the one human being
who could soothe the longing in her brittle heart.

Luke had warned him, and Fraser had been
watching for the lights. Now, as he moved forward in the moonlight, Kelly at his heels, he felt
as if his heart was going to burst from his chest.

'Here, girl. Stay.' He spoke softly to the dog as
he sheltered in the shadows of the trees that
bordered the properties.

Maddy.

He could see her on the verandah spotlit by
the glow that shone out from the living room
behind. Her head was lowered and buried in her
hands.

And he could hear something too. The faint
sound of her pain travelled through the still
evening air and found the target of his heart.

Oh, Maddy . . . My darling Maddy . . .

From where he stood in the darkness Fraser felt
himself overwhelmed by some elemental, mag-
netic force. His every instinct urged him to go to
her, take her in his arms, make her understand

that trust and love didn't have to end up in pain and suffering.

But, the thought choked him, Maddy Tyler was proud and vulnerable. No matter what he'd been told, he had no right to assume she would want him back in her life.

Beside him the dog whined and Fraser rested a cautioning hand on its warm head. For a moment longer he stared at the woman he loved, then turned and walked away into the night.

Maddy was up with the dawn, driven by the desire to do what needed to be done and be on her way. Close the door. Drive away. And spend the rest of her life trying to forget.

Only when the last of the cardboard boxes was taped and she was doing a final inspection of the rooms did she see the one object she'd forgotten.

The firescreen. She knew there was no way she could leave Fraser's gift to be sold with the house. It was too precious for that.

She could leave a note, she thought. Or tell the agent. Surely he could be trusted to see it was returned? It was Fraser's and he should have it back. A reminder of his past.

As she stood in that sun-filled room staring at the intricately wrought screen, Maddy succumbed to the sharp, breathless assault of the truth.

Fraser had given the screen to her. He had loved his wife so much, yet he had managed to move beyond the past . . .

And at that moment in time Maddy knew what she had come here for.

Fraser had glided fleetingly over the surface of sleep. When his gritty eyes flickered open he was aware of an almost physical pain at the knowledge that the woman he loved was so close by. And in a short time would be gone leaving him somehow to get through the rest of his life.

It was in those moments of awakening as he recalled the heartbreaking image of the night before that Fraser knew he would never be able to live with himself if he didn't give it one last try. He had seen her loneliness and vulnerability, had heard her suffering.

For all her protestations he knew without a doubt that Maddy Tyler needed what everyone needed.

Someone to love and trust. To comfort and understand.

He felt the drum-heavy thud in his chest as he rose and quickly headed for the shower. He had to give it one final chance.

And if she turned him away . . .? Well, at least he would know he had tried . . .

He decided to walk. Give himself time to think out exactly what he wanted to say, to make things as easy as possible. For both of them.

Grabbing his hat, and with Kelly eagerly scampering down the steps ahead of him, Fraser set out to cross the complex territory between Maddy Tyler and himself.

He was halfway across the back paddock when he saw her slim figure emerge from the trees on the property line.

She felt the tourniquet tighten around her heart as she caught sight of him. Heading directly towards her. The broad shoulders. The thick, greying hair under the same battered hat. Those wise, kind eyes . . .

'Fraser, I –'

But Kelly had rushed up and leapt on her, whimpering and whining in joyous recognition.

'Kelly! Down!' The dog took no notice of Fraser's command.

But Maddy was grateful for the distraction. She patted the excited, boisterous animal. 'It's okay . . . She remembers me. Good girl, Kelly . . . She's filled out, hasn't she?'

Their eyes met and Fraser saw the new lines on her thinner face.

'Maddy, I had to see you. Maybe you don't want to speak to me but –'

Up close she could see a subtle difference – some other, crueller, emotions had replaced the contentment and serenity she had once seen in his face.

'No, Fraser,' she interrupted him, 'I was on my way to see you. I just wanted to tell you that I'm leaving the fire-screen. And –' She broke off, her gaze locked on those blue, once sparkling eyes.

And as she looked into Fraser O'Neill's soul Maddy saw the damage she had done and understood the real reason for her final journey.

Only she was afraid it was too late.

For how could she ever make up to him for all the hurt and suffering, the pain and rejection, the ugly words . . .? But above all, how could she ever expect his forgiveness for not allowing him the chance to say goodbye to their child? For having missed those brief joyous hours of Francesca's life?

Tears welled into her eyes. She felt dizzy with the intensity of her longing to tell him how sorry she was, to reach out for him and hold him, try to make up for all she had cost him . . .

Then – the touch of a weather-worn hand on her arm, and through her tears Maddy realised that the expression had changed in those quiet, knowing eyes.

'Maddy . . . I understand . . .'

And then his arms were around her, drawing her close against the clamour of his heart, and Maddy clung to him, sobbing, and knew she was forgiven.

'Oh, Fraser . . . I need you. I really need you.'

The words that confronted her deepest fears.

'It's all right, Maddy. Everything's all right.'

CHAPTER TWENTY-ONE

It was almost a quarter of a century since Maddy Tyler had said the words 'I do' for the first time.

Now, as she stood in the garden she had created with the man who any moment would become her husband, she spoke those words again with a confidence and joy that resounded from her very soul.

She would take Fraser O'Neill to be her husband for better or worse. In sickness and in health. To love and to cherish . . . And in the face of all the Fates.

For life offers no guarantees and Maddy knew that marriage does not take away that essential aloneness which lies at the heart of every human being.

But she had grown strong in her tragedies, and the years had taught her many lessons. The greatest of which was to recognise love. And not be afraid.

The wedding had been arranged as quickly as possible given the fact that Christmas was almost upon them. But everyone was there – Jane and Luke, Tony, Del, Joy and her family, those in the town who had known Fraser O'Neill all his life, and those who had come to know Maddy Tyler. Even the real estate agent who had forgiven her for taking the cottage off the market. 'It'll belong to the O'Neills' again,' Maddy had explained softly. And like everyone else, he would soon find out about her plans to establish it as a gallery for local artists.

Now, as she stood beside Fraser in her cream lace dress, Maddy stood too at the edge of her new life. When the celebrant joined their hands as man and wife, she looked up into her second husband's wise and loving eyes. It still chilled her to think how close she had come to missing this. How blind she had been to the many different faces of love.

But the hand of God had cast its lot. And Maddy Tyler knew she was going to make the most of it.

Matthew Boulton

Library Resource Centre

Standard Loan	Telephone for renewals: **0121 446 4545 ext. 8036**

This is a 3 week loan and must be returned by the latest date shown below

10 Dec 08